The Glass Salamander

Books by Ann Downer

The Spellkey
The Glass Salamander

The Glass Salamander

by Ann Downer

Atheneum   1989   New York

Atheneum
Macmillan Publishing Company
866 Third Avenue, New York, NY 10022
Collier Macmillan Canada, Inc.
First Edition   Designed by Eliza Green
Printed in the United States of America

A Lucas/Evans Book

10 9 8 7 6 5 4 3 2 1

Library of Congress Cataloging-in-Publication Data
Downer, Ann.
The glass salamander / by Ann Downer—1st ed. p.   cm.
Summary: Caitlin's training as a seer on the Isle of Chameol is interrupted by the return
of the evil necromancer Myrrhlock, while her lost lover, the Badger,
investigates an outbreak of madness in two of the lower kingdoms. Sequel to
The Spellkey.
ISBN 0–689–31413–2
[1. Fantasy.] I. Title.   PZ7.D7575G1   1989   [Fic]—dc19
88–35034   CIP   AC

For Judy

For there is no friend like a sister. . . . To cheer one on the tedious way. . . .

Christina Rossetti, *Goblin Market*

Contents

The Choice

A tall, dark figure in a cape stood at the rail of the *Double Dolphin,* gazing out at the sea in a pose of princely meditation. Then the figure turned, swaying to keep balance on the deck of the pitching ship, and one could see it was a young woman, her hair cropped at the nape and curling softly in the salt wind off the sea. But what was most startling was the sight of her eyes, one blue and one green, set like jewels in her pale face, focused now on some scene only they could see, out over the waves.

What those remarkable eyes saw was a rider on a piebald horse, a golden head flashing between the white snow and the black trunks of winter trees. Lines, traces of harsh weather and harsh travel, made his young face seem older than it was. If his eyes saw some vision before them other than the snowy path, the rider's face did not betray it.

The young woman hung her head over the rail, suddenly dizzy, not from seasickness but a stab of loneliness. Though her eyes were the eyes of a seer, and the *Double Dolphin* was bearing her to Chameol and to an education as an oracle, the young woman had no idea when she would ever see the rider again.

It was only a few days ago that she had stood before the queen of Chameol, had stood before a choice.

"You may come to Chameol and be honored as our seer. All our secret arts will be open to you, and the ancient runebooks. You will be prepared to take your place as a high oracle. Or, if it is what you really want, your otherworld sight can be taken from you, and you may go back into the world as an ordinary woman. But if you choose Chameol, you must come alone."

Caitlin nodded. "Would I be blind, then, if I chose to remain in the world?"

"No, you would see and dream as other women do, but you would not be able to move between the dreamworld and the waking one as you do now." The queen of Chameol paused. "You would also lose all memory of what has happened, of me and of Chameol, and of the tanner's son. That will seem unduly cruel to you, but if you were allowed to remember even a little it would jeopardize our fight against Myrrhlock. The Badger is part of what you must forget if you do not choose to join us."

In the end, it had been no choice at all.

At the rail, the dark, caped figure raised her head and her eyes to the lead-colored sky.

"By that sweet heaven of yours, Badger, I wish I knew whether I'll ever see you again."

Far off, the rider on his piebald mount shivered. He had only just taken the vows of a knight of Chameol, thus surrendering his real name, his money and home, and the right ever to marry.

"It's not monkhood, mind," Elric had said. "It's just that you can never take a wife."

The Badger had nodded. He had no home and nothing to his name except his name; it had not been much to give up. If he could have, he would have surrendered his memory with it.

The Haunting, or
What Ailed Him

Sleep, when it came to the Badger at all, was at best a
catnap from which he woke stiff and cursing, at worst a
night's vigil spent wrestling with demons.

Every night it was the same. He had tried gin, a tea brewed
of poppies, even the weird, aromatic pipe of mandrake. He
had cast himself like a man shipwrecked on the shores of
a countess's bed, followed inkeepers' daughters up the lad-
der to the loft as if to oblivion. He haunted the alleys where
half-witches sold spells of forgetfulness; on their counsel
he had begged a cup of madmen's piss from the keeper at
the asylum gate, had drunk it down with the ashes from a
lock of hair. When he had retched the foul toddy up again
he swore off debauchery and took up self-denial, going for
days without water, food, or sleep, shaving his head so that
only a rough gilt glittered on his scalp and chin.

But every night it was the same, and this night no different
from the others. As soon as his eyes closed in sleep, the
ghost came to spoil his rest, so that he woke in a sweat,
damning the name and face of her who would give him no
peace.

Elric watched this and said nothing. What good would it
do to say forget her, when the wretch would sell his soul
to do that very thing? So, for the time being, Elric suffered
the Badger his exotics and purgatives. After all, hadn't there
been a time when he had done the same himself? And, too,
the elder man wondered how much the younger one really

wanted to forget her, for around his wrist the Badger wore still a braided circlet of that matchless ebony-and-indigo hair.

It was odd to think that only a few months ago circumstances had found the companions in a convent far to the north, playing a dire game of cat-and-mouse through the stalls and lofts of the temple. He had found himself, Elric remembered, in a nun's habit, the Badger's knife poised at his throat. That misunderstanding had been cleared up, and they had now spent nine months in the saddle, the Badger playing pupil to Elric's tutor, learning the arts of disguise and artifice that were their trade and profession.

Some knights there were, the Badger knew, who studied archery, falconry, and fencing. "No such education for you," Elric had said, setting the Badger to work by the fire with pots of paint, black and white and red, to change himself from horse thief to innkeeper to prince and back again. He taught the Badger to mix the uncanny, unreliable potion that could change his blue eyes to black or merely make him sick as a dog. Other times Elric would lounge by the fire, a switch in one hand, while the Badger stood stork-fashion on a nearby anthill. At the slightest movement of the Badger's foot, Elric would tap the anthill with the wand to excite the red swarm within. A variation of this exercise involved painting the Badger's upper lip with honey and bidding him sit impassive while the wasps came to collect it.

"Torturer," the Badger muttered once, early on, through a badly swollen lip.

"Not at all," Elric said, lighting his pipe and offering the Badger a clove poultice in a red-checkered handkerchief. "You must learn these things, absorb them utterly, or the lack of them could kill you. A twitch of the lip, a sneeze, a careless footfall could be your undoing. We're the opposite of most knights, you and I. We can't wear our colors for all to see."

Now they were journeying through the fens and marshes of Oncemoon, where there had been reports of hauntings of another kind. Word had reached Chameol of a merchant, respected in the town for his sobriety, who had fastened a live piglet to his head and insisted it was a hat. In another incident, a judge had sealed the windows and door of her house with pastry while her family slept. More cause for amusement than alarm, except for the young girl, clad in nothing but swanthistle and rushflower, who had wandered off into the marsh and was presumed drowned. Indeed, most of the sufferers seemed to be children: Reports had reached Chameol of children worried and bitten by unseen demons. Iiliana, Queen of Chameol, had dispatched the two knights to see what could be made of it.

They were ready to set out when Elric found the Badger, his head wrapped in buttered cheesecloth, about to lay his head on the hot coals and "roast the ghost out," and realized things had gone far enough.

"Come on," he said, hauling the Badger to his feet and unwinding the turban, "you're no good to me if your brain's been roasted like a chestnut."

Elric knew a conjurer who lived in the marsh, and he brought the Badger to her, careful to let him think it was their mission for Chameol that called them there.

Grisaudra watched Elric row the boat toward the small island where a hut accommodated herself, a cat, and some wild pigs trained to nose out edible roots from the marsh. The conjurer of Oncemoon Marsh was ugly, not in a manner to arouse disgust, but because she came so close to being not ugly at all. She was wraith-thin, an urchin's height, with hair grey before its time that stood up along her scalp as if singed. One eye, through birth or accident, was swollen shut, the other was peculiarly clear and bright, as if it held the vision of both. Grisaudra had taken the blade of a sword in the face as a girl and lived, and the scar cleft her mouth from ear to chin.

But the sorcerer's voice made up for all that, a sweet, sad music that had once brought tears to an executioner's eyes. It was a pity, Elric thought, that Grisaudra of Oncemoon Marsh did not say much. A blind man or two might have fallen in love with her.

Grisaudra nodded without really listening to the Badger's inquiries about the drowned girl. While the Badger was making fast the boat, Elric had slipped into the hut to whisper his real purpose in coming. Now Grisaudra studied her patient with interest, noting the haunted stare of the eyes without seeing their fetching blue. She read the Badger's eyes for a long moment, as if gathering from their depths the particulars she needed for this illusion. Then, turning to the fire, Grisaudra spoke.

"I didn't see the girl you describe. Wearing only swan-thistle, you say? Too prickly a petticoat, to my taste." With her back turned, Grisaudra quietly took up a wand of birch-wood. She struck the side of the chimney with it, and a fluttering, batlike cloud of soot flew into the Badger's face. From her pocket, Grisaudra removed a droppered vial of mixed venom, blood, and tears. The Badger tried to twist away as she seized his head in a purposeful grip.

"What's that?"

"Salve for the sting. Look up."

Coughing and rubbing his eyes, the Badger allowed the conjurer to minister to him. Grisaudra put a hand to the side of the Badger's head, steadying it for the drops, her palm slyly reading the knobs of his skull, the ledger of his memory.

Elric drew into the corner. He had seen this once before, and the memory still made him shiver. The smoke clung only to the Badger's face, leaving Elric's eyes clear to take in the unfolding scene.

The Badger swore as the drops went in, trying to dash the stinging stuff away. Then, through the rosy film in his eyes, he got a look at Grisaudra and blinked in disbelief. He murmured a name and with it something between a curse and a prayer, putting out a hand and raking his fingers through the air by Grisaudra's shoulders, as though something lay there, heavy and indigo, besides her rough garment. Grisaudra let herself be pulled into his arms and struggled for only a moment before she let the Badger close the inch that separated his mouth from hers.

Before she came to the marsh Grisaudra had made her home among a troupe of vagabond actors and acrobats and, before that, dressed as a boy, among the hired swords of the border wars of Tenthmoon. It was as much her dramatics as the drops that enabled her to work her magic. Seeing her from behind, as the Badger spread his cloak on the rush floor of the hut, even Elric could believe she was Caitlin.

Elric went outside to have a pipe. It was more morning than night when Grisaudra finally joined him. He passed her the pipe, for which she was grateful.

"He'll sleep now, ten hours, I'd say, maybe more." She darted him a glance through a wreath of clove smoke. "It'll be extra this time, you know. Triple for anything past a kiss—and it went rather beyond that."

"Of course," Elric said.

Her eyes were off, through the bracken to the moon. "Well, you know how I dislike it. Besides, my shirt's rent." She squared her thin shoulders against some memory, or against the chill. It occurred to Elric that the welt on her face was the least of Grisaudra's scars.

When the Badger awoke, he showed no surprise at finding himself in Grisaudra's hut, no memory of his delusion of the day before, and no trace of his past ailment. He gave Grisaudra a piece of silver in payment for bed and breakfast, which made her color with embarrassment. While those dosed with the drops were usually content merely to gaze upon their heart's desire, Grisaudra more than occasionally was called to lay down her body to effect a cure. It was all right in her mind, as long as the "sufferers," as she thought of them, did not pay her. When the Badger had gone outside to untie the boat, Grisaudra pressed the money into Elric's hand. He took it without saying a word, but later, when she had watched the boat disappear into the mists, Grisaudra found another coin in the corner, beneath her sleeping cat.

That night, as she slept alone, strange visions from her patient's memory played themselves out in her dreams. A young woman, hair cropped and dressed for hard riding, knelt in the surf at the base of a cliff. The same figure, but her hair past her waist this time, wearing a collar and manacles of bells. And again, sitting in a marble hall in a dress of yellow silk, a litter of cats in her lap.

Grisaudra rose and lit a lamp of firefly weed. In the greenish light it gave she roused yesterday's fire and, when the kettle boiled, brewed some sage tea—good for disorders of the brain and trembling of the limbs. She went back to bed and indeed dreamed no more that night, lying awake instead, feeling all over again the desperate embrace, the rasp of his unshaven chin on her throat, and how hot she had felt, there on the cold rush floor.

Grisaudra rubbed her head; all entwined, they had rolled under the table, and she had cracked her noggin. Funny, she hadn't felt it at the time. Now she was going to have a nice, egg-sized lump there. Silly fellow! Whatever had there been for him to cry about, afterward, until he fell asleep in her arms?

The two knights reined in their horses and asked directions of some children who were swarming over the roof of a house.

Elric hefted his purse. "There's something in here for the one who can tell me the way to the shoemaker."

A freckled girl with skinned knees shinnied down the waterspout, barely on the ground before her hand was out for payment.

"It's down the hill, by the granary what was all burned up." Seeing that the purse was not forthcoming, the girl hopped from foot to foot impatiently and added hopefully, "It's an old brick house, you'll see, with green shutters." This won her the purse and the half pound of lemon drops inside, gold enough to make her the richest child there—and to make her lose interest instantly and completely in pastry, even if it did come from the roof of a house.

They found the shoemaker's by following the smell of wet ashes. Three doors down from the burned-out shell of the granary, they turned in at a house with green shutters and a shingle in the shape of a shoe.

By the fire an aproned woman sat bent over her work. The Badger called out, "Will you tell the cobbler we are here to see him?"

The woman turned, and they saw she wore an apron of leather, and that she held not her darning, but a last and awl.

"When I was made a widow, I was made a cobbler, too," she said, setting the half-finished shoe down on the bench and waving a hand to some chairs. "Forgive me: I have given up more wifely things; I think I can still boil water. Can I give you a cup of something hot?"

A teapot was hunted up that, when the dust was washed off, revealed itself to be blue. The cobbler considered the

Badger's question, or she might have been reading the pattern of leaves swirling in the hot water. As if to put a lid on her thoughts, she quickly covered the teapot and poured out the tea, answering.

"It was the geese we noticed first. Or Tillie noticed them, running around the yard as if a fox, or a fox from hell, were after them. The next day the whole flock was dead.

"Then we all came down with the fever. And Tillie nursed us all. I helped with the sheets and the gruel, until I came down with it, too. When the fever finally broke, she was gone. Someone had seen her wandering in the marsh, it seems." The cobbler laughed, put up a hand to cover a crooked smile, her eyes bright with tears.

"My Tilda! You never saw a child more sober, as practical, less given to fancy. And beautiful—what puzzles me is, if she was wearing nothing but some thistledown when she walked into the marsh, why half the men in the county didn't walk in after her."

The cobbler suddenly gave a cry and dropped the piece of leather she had been holding. She had not been working her shoemaker's awl into the leather, as she meant to, but into the flesh of her palm.

How will she manage now, Elric wondered as they left her, her hand bandaged, staring into the fire. The Badger cursed, spun on his heel, and went back into the house.

"Forgive me—I would not press you except that it may prove useful. How did your husband die?"

The woman looked up. "Fighting the fire in the granary, last harvest. And what have we had since then but rain?"

The Badger could bring himself to ask her no more questions, only drew the wine within her reach, as she asked, and left her.

After he had swung into the saddle, they rode awhile in silence.

"What an awful thing," the Badger said at last, "to lose first one to fire and another to water."

They doubled back to the judge's house, where the beleaguered husband had just chased the last of the children off the roof with a broom and a volley of coal. His wife, he told them, was greatly improved.

"She's finally gone off to sleep—three weeks without so much as a wink, and if she wasn't plastering the roof or painting the floors with almond water and egg white, singing hey-nonny-non, and then hey-nonny *back*ward . . ." The judge's husband leaned on the broom handle. "We've only just got the youngest unsewn from the cradle. And the smell. We haven't been able to get it out of the house."

"A smell?" asked Elric.

"Well, I hate to say it. You see, normally my wife is the sweetest of women, and sweet smelling. But the whole time she was ailing she sweated like a blacksmith. It ran off her— we had to change her bedclothes every hour, and I had to boil them to get the smell out. Like dead mice, dead mice in a chamber pot."

"This lasted three weeks?"

"Yes. It began just after the harvest. The town council had just sent over her salary, a sack of grain for the next quarter. I remember, she complained it seemed like sweepings off the threshing floor. My wife is a very particular woman."

"What to make of it?"

The knights had made their way to the town's only tavern, the Bandit's Thumb. The mulled ale could not totally dispel the chill that gripped the Badger as he thought of the waters of the marsh closing over the girl's eyes, over her mouth.

Elric shook his head. "I can't say I see any diabolical agent at work. But I can't believe they all took leave of their senses out of coincidence."

"They all said the same thing: the sleeplessness, burning

and freezing by turns, hallucinations. Some*one* or some-*thing* is at work in it. I just don't understand how it could affect them all so differently and not touch the rest of the household."

"There's something we don't know yet, a missing piece. Here—there've been some reports in Twinmoon. Perhaps we'll learn what we need there."

The two knights rode out along the high road, the Badger on the piebald, Motley, Elric on a roan mare. One of the carts bound for market caught the Badger's eye; there was something about its cargo. Nothing amiss, really, just very odd. It was the way the sacks were piled strangely upright in almost human forms, and the strange way the driver sat, as if he were Death himself.

As their horses drew alongside the cart, the Badger had to laugh at himself. They weren't sacks of grain after all, or not all of them. They were beggars in sackcloth.

"Lepers," said Elric. He chirruped to his mount and urged her forward with his heels, and the Badger followed, as Elric had meant him to. It would do no good, the red-haired knight had thought, for the Badger to look too hard. Each of the lepers wore a bell fastened around the neck, and the last thing Elric wanted was for the Badger to relapse into his haunted state.

But Elric was wrong after all. They were not bells but small, hollow globes of blue glass. And whatever else the silent figures in sackcloth were, they were not lepers. The cart hit a rut in the road, and the jolt loosened the hood of one of the silent human cargo. The hood fell back to reveal a face unmarred by leprous lesions, a face so uncommonly beautiful that if its owner had walked into Oncemoon Marsh, a man would like as not walk in after her. Her hair was the color of clouded honey, and there were broken twigs of swanthistle caught in it.

The driver was gaunt and grim-faced, his countenance remarkable for the utter coldness of its eyes and the harelip that split the mouth. He turned in his seat, barely taking his eyes from the road, and raised the hood once more so that the face and its beauty were eclipsed by sackcloth. Then the cart and its strange freight continued on into Twinmoon.

The Secret, or
What Caitlin Knew

*T*he Queen of Chameol sat on her balcony, her bronze hair falling out of the braided circlet that was her only crown. A small table on her left held sealing wax, a paper knife, an inkwell, and a mound of unanswered messages. A twin table on her right held her cold tea and some fruit, bitten once and forgotten. Iiliana gazed out over the orchards to the sea, absently stroking a bird in her lap, the pigeon that had brought her morning's mail.

In the distance, off the swells where the sea-flax grew, Iiliana could see bobbing a dozen or so sleek black floats of the kind the fishermen used to mark their nets. Iiliana sat up straighter, then rang a little bell on the left-hand table. A young girl appeared silently in the doorway.

"Fetch my spyglass," Iiliana ordered, "and here—take this." She pressed the pigeon into the girl's hands.

A few moments later Iiliana lowered the spyglass with a low *yes!* of triumph. The seals had returned from their winter pastures in other waters to birth their pups in the seas off Chameol. Iiliana threw off her shawl and drew on a heavy, waterproof cloak.

"Maarta, Iida, come quickly! And Iilsa, put on a kettle of soup. You had better make it fish," she shouted back over her shoulder, already running down to the beach.

As the queen and her handwomen goat-stepped down the slick stairs carved out of the cliff face, they could see that one of the seals had separated from the rest and was swimming toward the rocky surf. A cry reached them, half seal bark, half human laughter. The seal cleared the sharp rocks with inborn skill, then collapsed in the shallows, suddenly helpless and clumsy out of the water.

Iiliana reached the creature first. It seemed to have been deformed by some accident, its flippers and tail misshapen, torn in a net or in a sea dragon's jaws. The seal raised its head and gave Iiliana a knowing look. It had human eyes, one blue as the sky, one green as the sea. Iiliana knelt by it and with a knife began to cut through the gleaming black-and-silver pelt.

And it was not a seal, after all, but a young woman. Under the tar that coated her face she was naturally pale, made unnaturally so by her winter's sojourn in the cold sea with the seals. She had been sewn into a seal's pelt tighter than her own skin, a layer of mutton fat her only undergarment. The reek was fierce. They washed her there on the beach and threw her chattering into a heavy woolen robe before hauling her up in a pulley and basket to the top of the cliff, where a wagon was waiting.

They brought her back to the modest low white buildings that were the island's palace. There Caitlin was fed hot soup, which Iiliana had to send back for more crab claws and fish heads before it would suit Caitlin's seal tastes. It took a week before her seal voice began to fade and they could again fathom her speech, and even then, when extraordinarily excited or amused, she would now and again lapse into barking.

At the end of the week Iiliana appeared in Caitlin's room with a strange parcel: two large shells bound in sea-flax.

"This was left for you on the beach."

Caitlin turned the contents out into her lap: some iridescent fish scales; a piece of black coral polished by the sea into the shape of a seal; some coins crusted green, kings made into ogres by time and salt water. Curious, Iiliana reached over and turned over one last object. It alone was not of the sea, and it alone was unchanged by it: a long-dead glassworker's brag-piece, a glass salamander, all red-and-purple transparency, curled in on itself as if in sleep.

"This is from the Elder Age," Iiliana said.

Caitlin nodded, rubbing the glass so it winked. Her own treasure, a cat amulet, had been lost in the sea. "It's a seer's glass."

Caitlin had come to Chameol to become a seer. Raised by a witch in the heart of the Weirdwood, Caitlin had endured a cat's belling at the hands of villagers, spending the remainder of her girlhood on a barren moor, making her home in an ancient warrior's barrow.

Her promise had survived all that, had survived trials at the hands of the ancient and powerful necromancer, Myrrhlock, though for her first weeks at Chameol, Caitlin had left a light burning all night beside her bed.

When the night terrors had ceased, Iiliana had summoned Caitlin to begin her apprenticeship, the honing of her gift. In the beginning, Caitlin had had her doubts.

"You want me to make *cheese*?"

Iiliana's laughter had pealed in the underground chamber.

"Don't tell me you've never divined with cheeses? Oh, someone, hand her a dowsing fork, and we'll dig a well of buttermilk!" The queen sat on a barrel, chuckling.

Caitlin put her hands on her hips. "Well, what am I supposed to think?" Iiliana had wakened her at dawn, bade her put on a smock and tie her head in a white cloth, and handed her a small, curved knife, for all the world as if they were going to cut mistletoe.

"The cloth is to keep your hair out of the milk, and the knife's for tasting. Here, work at this a few weeks, and if you can in truth tell me you've learned nothing worthwhile, you can stop."

For a month, then, she had labored in the cheese caverns, learning to mix the milk and rennet, to salt and strain the curd, to know by a rap of her knuckles on a red wheel of cheese if it was ready to be rolled up out of the dark to the table. One day Caitlin cast off the smock and kerchief and went knocking at Iiliana's door.

"I have had enough."

Iiliana was at her sewing; her shears made a light, disapproving click as she set them down. "Oh? What makes you think so?"

"This morning I found myself talking to a cheese."

"And? Did it answer you?"

"It's funny—it did, in its way." Caitlin had long divined with candle wax in a basin of water, but in her lonely weeks alone underground she had started to see runes everywhere, in the swirling milk as she stirred it, in the curds that formed, in the red-and-black wax in which she enrobed the great wheels. They had spelled out her secret, declared the thing that she must, for now, tell no one.

"What am I to try next?" she asked Iiliana. "Wine making?"

"Not quite." And Iiliana had held up to the light the glossy sealskin.

From Caitlin's window there was no sign of the storms that had worried the straits of Chameol all winter. From the balcony of her bedchamber she could see the fleecy waves skip to the base of the cliff and back again, like the lambs in the meadows above. The trees of the orchards were lively with birds, and there were new foals among the herd of wild horses that came by moonlight to graze on the salt grass. In the greying of the night Caitlin woke to the wickering of mare to colt. Once she was roused, the smell of the night-blooming vine outside her window kept her awake until dawn.

For spring had not come to Caitlin's heart; it was heavy and cold, cracked open with swelling ice. She could not seem to get warm, even on these balmy nights, and when she pressed a hand to her heart it felt sore. She did not try any of the remedies, the herbs and charms, at her disposal. She knew what ailed her, knew where the cure lay, knew the cure was the one thing she could never seek out. How could she forget the Badger, when every day her body was being remade with the memory of him?

Among the seals, she had felt some relief. Anchored fast in a bed of sea-flax among the sleeping clan, she had forgotten human speech, had dreamed seal dreams. One of the seals had become as infatuated with her as any human lover and was not content unless Caitlin took fish from his mouth and slept all night beneath the watery stars, clinging fast to his fur, her face pressed to his bristly cheek. Now when she walked along the beach, Caitlin could hear him crying, calling for her in the seal name she had taken. Sometimes, in her dreams, Caitlin was in the Badger's arms again, but he had a seal's face. Just as often she clung in her dreams to the seal, only to have him turn on her a blue-eyed, human gaze.

Caitlin turned from the window and peevishly took up her hairbrush, lashing at her hair as if she meant to teach it a lesson. With each stroke she muttered a charm, a spell for lengthening, but she forgot to say a charm against tangles. Her brush caught on a snarl and with an oath Caitlin hurled the brush at the door.

It missed Iiliana by a hair's breadth. With a cluck of her tongue the bronze-haired queen of Chameol shook the ivory brush at her apprentice.

"Now, now! You know the rules! No spell casting during your probation, not even to make your hair grow faster."

Caitlin turned away with a scowl and quickly drew on a robe to hide her softly swelling middle from Iiliana's sharp eyes. She had been lucky no one had noticed on the beach, when they had cut her out of the sealskin. But already she thought her tutor was suspicious of Caitlin's newfound passion for cake and sweets, her sudden loathing of being attended when she dressed and bathed.

Iiliana looked thoughtfully at her young oracle-in-the-making. "We'll skip your archery and geometry this morning. I think the best thing for you would be a nice, lazy breakfast in the garden."

Under the spreading branches of a tree in bloom, Iiliana pulled Caitlin's favorite chair into a sun-dappled spot and piled it high with cushions. Once Caitlin was settled, Iiliana produced bowls of scalding tea, a platter of buttered toast, and a covered dish. Her stomach had been fickle lately, but suddenly Caitlin was starving.

"Ah—that smells wonderful. What is it?"

Iiliana whisked the cover away to reveal calves' brains and pigs' feet on a bed of tripe. Caitlin sprang up with a cry of disgust, but the wave of nausea beat her to the hedge. For several minutes she was violently sick. Iiliana silently chafed her wrists and, when Caitlin seemed somewhat recovered, helped her back to her chair. Someone had removed the covered dish. Iiliana seized Caitlin's chin and turned her face gently, but firmly, to her own.

"How far gone?"

Caitlin twisted away. "I don't know what you mean."

"Oh, but I think you do, my girl. I wasn't sure until this morning, and even then I thought we'd better have a little test. Normally, you have a cool enough head and a strong enough stomach. But then, things aren't quite normal with you, are they?"

Caitlin sighed. "About four months, by my reckoning."

Iiliana nodded thoughtfully. "Will you tell him?"

Caitlin folded a napkin into smaller and smaller triangles. "How can I?"

"He could be found, if that was what you wanted. But that is not what I asked you."

There were no men on Chameol; the price of becoming

a seer had been to leave her past, and the Badger, behind.

"And if it is a boy?" Caitlin said, lifting her head. "Will you put him off the island, to live with the seals?"

"You know the answer to that as well as I do." No boy was made to leave his mother until his voice had changed.

Caitlin fell silent. She did not tell Iiliana that, gazing into the salamander glass, she had seen a fine, black-haired baby boy, that she had next seen an empty cradle.

It was harvest time once more when she was delivered of her son. Iiliana placed him, black-headed as a seal, in Caitlin's arms. He howled. Iiliana beamed and covered her ears.

"Ah, what a wonderful racket."

Caitlin smiled. "He favors his father in that, at least."

The child had his mother's dark looks but not, to Caitlin's relief, her seer's eyes.

"They're almost always passed from mother to daughter," Iiliana said. She was braiding Caitlin's hair into a heavy rope, weaving in a silver ribbon as she went. The child slept in a basket at Caitlin's feet. He was three weeks old, and she had not been able to settle on a suitable name. It had become a great contest among everyone on the island. Caitlin was opening dozens of the paper twists that collected every day in a designated jar outside the buttery.

"Ugh," she said, tossing them into the fire as she went. With one foot she jiggled the basket lightly. "Listen to these! Derward, Galt, Adalard. Sweet heaven, what names!"

An old woman drew near. She was new to the island; her fisherman husband, sorely tried by her quarrelsomeness, had set her adrift. Her face was red without being rosy, her hands sharp without being nimble. She burned the bread and the shirts alike and was as useless at gardening as she was at weaving. At last, out of desperation more than pity,

Caitlin had agreed to have her as a maid while the child was nursing. The old woman squeezed one of her pawlike hands into the jar and drew out a paper twist. It had a singed look, as if it had been snatched out of the ashes, where Caitlin had thrown it. Oh, why wound her feelings, Caitlin thought. It can't hurt to read it again. She opened the paper twist.

"Bram," she read.

"A little black bird," Iiliana said, taking the paper from Caitlin's hand. "That he is, certainly." The queen of Chameol wrinkled her brow. *Bram.* It meant a black bird, but whether a black bird or a crow, Iiliana couldn't remember. It meant something, if she could only remember what. There was a book in the library somewhere, if she could put her hands on it. The makeshift nursemaid had put in a stint there, too, more's the pity, and Iiliana was not at all sure where the book of names was. But what did it matter? Looking at Caitlin's face, Iiliana could see the matter was settled, and she swallowed the mild caution that had been on her lips.

Caitlin jiggled the basket with her foot. "Well, what do you think, my fellow? Are you a Bram?" The baby opened his eyes and gazed solemnly at his mother. She lifted him out to kiss him. Bram, she thought. Bram. She laughed sheepishly.

"How silly—but he's quite simply a Bram."

The old woman laughed and showed her bad teeth. She picked some hot cinders out of the fire, even though they burned her fingers; she used them to singe the hairs on her chin. The old woman's name, which no one could seem to remember, was Ordella, an elf-sword, something other-worldly and sharp.

Caitlin woke the next morning with the feeling that something was wrong. She lay in bed, listening for a moment before she realized Bram had not cried to be fed. That old woman, Caitlin thought, has been giving him a sugar teat, and I've told her time and time again she's not to.

She got out of bed and got the baby from his cradle. "Look at you," she said, shaking her head. "That Ordella's got you swaddled so tight you look like a loaf of bread from the baker." She unwrapped his dark head and put him to her breast.

But it wasn't Bram. It was a goblin baby. Its ears were pointed, its complexion a little too ruddy, but most of all it had yellow cat's eyes and small, sharp teeth. It did not cry but regarded her with a goblin's dispassion through large eyes of molten gold.

The household was roused and the palace searched, but Ordella had vanished without a trace. It was remembered that when she had been discovered adrift in the fishing boat, Ordella had in her possession a wicker eel trap, just the size for concealing a goblin child. Iiliana received the news grimly, her eyes red-rimmed. A little sweet gum and thistle to pacify the baby, and no one would think to search an eel trap.

Caitlin herself was beyond tears. She stood looking at the changeling, where it lay in Bram's basket, and terror seized her heart. Will they keep him warm? How will they feed him? she wondered.

"How will we feed him?" she heard herself say aloud.

Iiliana looked at her strangely. "It will take milk, if it can get it. But it would be better to give it a little beef broth. It's not a human child, Caitlin. It's not of this world at all. You must be careful of it."

When some broth had been warmed and brought, Caitlin reached over and removed the thistle teat from the changeling's mouth. Somehow, she thought it would not bite.

Changelings

*E*very morning, when the first pale bars of light slanted through the shutters and fell on her pillow, Caitlin would rise sleepless from her bed. Silently and swiftly she dressed, slipped the glass salamander into the pocket of her cloak, and stepped over the mastiff asleep in her doorway.

Over the fields she went, through the high salt grass wet with mist, following the sighing of the waves down to the sea. There, for hours on end, she remained as motionless as the rock on which she sat, deaf to everything but the surf on the rocks, blind to everything but the seer's glass she held cupped in her hands.

For a long string of days the glass refused to speak. Caitlin began to think her seer's gift was gone, lost to her now as the seal's speech that mocked her. Perhaps it was not a real seer's glass after all, but a clever fraud; after all, the Elder Age had had its talented swindlers along with its skilled artisans. One morning Caitlin's patience came to an end, and she raised her hand, poised to return the seer's glass to the waves that had given it up.

"It seems you speak only to seals. Well, they can have you!"

The vision struck her with the force of an icy wave so that she nearly dropped the salamander. What the seer's glass chose to show her at long last was Bram, cradled in a pair of arms. But they were not the arms of the Necromancer, at least not Myrrhlock in any shape he liked to take. These arms seemed living marble, pale and cold as frost on glass, bones as light and small as a hummingbird's—and were those *wings* behind?

Caitlin leaped up from the rock, the wind tugging back the hood of her cloak, setting her hair leaping about her face like an unruly dog, dark and sleek. The wind tore her voice from her throat as she let loose a shout of twin relief and frustration. Myrrhlock didn't have Bram—but who did?

Iiliana listened carefully as Caitlin related the vision the glass salamander had shown her. When she had finished, the queen of Chameol sat a moment in silence, as if a stone weighed on her tongue and made it too heavy for speech. At last she sighed and spoke.

"Caitlin, how much sleep have you gotten since Bram was taken?"

"What has that got to do with it?" Caitlin's color was already high from the salt air, her hair wild around her face, and she pushed it back, suddenly aware that she must look and sound more than a little like a frantic mother gone mad. "So you think this is all a fantasy brought on by too much worry and too little sleep?"

Iiliana smiled and shook her head, putting up a hand to smooth the furrows from Caitlin's brow. "No one is denying your seer's gift. But you must question whether you are summoning what you want your eyes to show you. Myrrhlock was nearly destroyed by you. We know he is abroad again. We have reports of his doings. In his weakened state he dares not strike at you. But your child: That is another matter; that would be a sweet revenge indeed. Does it matter in the end whether the agent was Ordella or this creature with wings?" Iiliana's mouth trembled, and her eyes were bright as she gripped Caitlin's hand. "I am afraid, Caitlin, very much afraid that Bram is—gone."

By its very nature, Chameol was an island of misfits, a place where a woman the outside world had deemed mad might find herself not only believed but honored as a seer, where a lonely recluse could work the herb beds or tend the beehives in peace. Widows with no one left to them in all the world could find contentment tending the flocks of goats or transcribing the songs of birds.

The cases of the younger islanders were somewhat different. Often they had made a misstart in life, destined to scrape a living from the gutters and alleys of the towns, until at last they had the luck to run afoul of a knight of Chameol.

Thus Midge had come to Chameol. Her brothers had given her the name because "she buzzed in your ears and bit." At seven, she was already an experienced pickpocket. That particular morning she had been working the flophouses, where beggars and drunks could buy a bed of clean straw for six coppers, day-old straw for three. Pickings were slim, unless you knew where to look. She spied a man whose clothes, beneath the dirt, were finely made and whose snoring showed the glint of a gold molar: a gambler who might still have some of his winnings on him. She slipped her hand into the pocket of his vest only to find her wrist seized in an iron grip.

Instead of turning her in, he had bought her a currant bun and a pint of milk and a ten-copper hot bath at an inn. A woman brought her clean clothes and a heavy cloak. By evening, she was asleep in a small fishing boat under the stars. And in the morning, she had awakened on Chameol.

On the island she was called by her real name, though they spelled it Chameol-fashion: Iimogen. In the beginning she missed the clamor of street life and old deaf Mistress Peekie, who ran the flophouse. And she missed her lame tabby cat, the one that used to hold a live cricket gently between its paws just to hear it sing. But the island grew on her: a field of white daisies basking in moonlight, baby goats romping on the hillside, the dolphins. Iimogen woke one morning with a strange feeling and spent the whole morning doing her chores, wondering whether she was getting the flu. Then she realized what it was: She was happy.

And so she had been for seven years, until she turned fourteen and came into the awkwardness. Suddenly she seemed to be all elbows and knees and couldn't move without knocking over something or hitting her funny bone.

It was her turn that year to enter the lottery for tasks on the island that required new hands. Iimogen seemed to have a talent for none of the arts prized on Chameol, and when she drew a high number in the lottery her name went to the bottom of the list of those waiting to become dolphin keepers. Iimogen sighed when she thought of her lottery number. Eighty-nine! She would be raking sea-flax until she herself was eighty-nine before she ever became a dolphin keeper.

Then Iiliana herself had summoned her, and Iimogen had been told she was to be sent away, if she liked, to be trained to be something quite different: a page of Chameol. The knight who had brought her to Chameol seven years before had remembered and recommended her. So Iimogen went away in a boat with nothing but the clothes on her back.

What a blow it had been, after all, to find that the camp was no different from Chameol and that she was just as hopeless at the new chores she was given to do. She had unlearned her pickpocket's skills too well and seemed unable to summon them back now that they were wanted again. Not even in this way could she be useful! Iimogen feared she would be sent back to Iiliana in disgrace.

One night Iimogen slipped from her bunk, took her bundle from its hiding place, freed a pigeon cage from its hook, and crept out into the cool darkness. Some of her lessons, at least, she had learned well; she woke no one. Outside, she crouched in the shadows and considered her next move; she could not go back to Chameol, so it would be back to the alley, and to Mistress Peekie. The pigeon would take word to Chameol, once she was safely away, to tell them not to worry.

The town road was empty in the slowly lightening darkness. The first wagon to pass was not headed to market; the sides were red and bore a picture of a fierce lion and the words ROLLO THE GREAT. The second wagon, also red, was painted with a picture of a man eating a fiery brand. From this cart there issued sleepy banter and sweet pipe smoke that made Iimogen pause, weighing whether to try her luck with the troupe of players. Then she saw the third wagon, grey as the dawn, piled with sacks of grain. Without a noise, Iimogen pulled herself aboard.

It was not long before she realized her grave mistake. The sacks held not meal but still, silent figures that looked right through her with the eyes of ghosts. Iimogen did not cry out, and made no sound to give herself away, crouching among the sacks. The knights had taught her how to write a message in the dark, using a pin for her pen. Iimogen pricked her fingers as often as the paper in her dread and haste, but the message took shape, and it was only a matter of fastening the capsule to the bird's leg. Then, with a thudding heart she felt the cart stop, heard the driver's footsteps approach the back of the cart. From the shadowy depths of a hood, cold eyes picked her out from among the rest in their sackcloth and eerie glass bells.

"What have we here, a runaway? Or something more?" The eyes, pale but cold and lightless, turned their gaze to the small cage Iimogen clutched in her lap. "What do you have there?"

"A—a bird. Please—it's just my pet," she stammered.

"More than a pet, I think. A pigeon. The very sort Iiliana

favors as her messenger." The icy gaze turned up again, to search Iimogen's face. "A girl, in truth. For a moment I thought you just a reckless boy. Iiliana is choosing her pages younger and younger these days."

His hand reached for the bird, but not before Iimogen had flung it away. As the knights had taught her, she had weakened the catch with careful twisting, and the cage broke open in the road. The bird was off like a stone from a slingshot.

The cold, bloodless hand closed on Iimogen's throat, and she was sure he meant to throttle her, but it was only to fasten on a collar with a glowing bell of blue glass.

The pigeon winged its way homeward to the dovecote on the Chameol palace roof. The old woman who kept the pigeons tended to this latest arrival, giving the bird its fill of seed and water before removing the leg capsule and sending the message down to the queen's chambers with the rest of the morning's mail.

Iiliana read the topmost message and pushed the rest of the pile away. Caitlin glanced up from her book by the window.

"Bad news?"

"Of a kind." Iiliana silently held out the message. Caitlin took the slip and read: HELP TWINMOON RED WAGONS.

Caitlin furrowed her brow. "It's not signed. And written with a pin it's hard to tell whether it's Elric's hand or the Badger's."

"Neither, I think—the mark of a child is strong both in the words chosen and the way the pin formed them."

Caitlin remembered the message recently received from the school for would-be knights. "You think it is from Iimogen?"

"I fear it is." Iiliana rose from her chair and began to pace. "Red wagons! Red Wagons! What on earth can she mean?"

"Do you think she was watched as she wrote it?"

"Oh no. Myrrhlock would never have let her finish it, much less let the bird get past the sill. No, Iimogen is a very literal-minded child, when her head's not clouded with fantasies of derring-do. If she said red wagons she meant red wagons."

Caitlin pressed her hands to her temples, remembering a marketplace and a smell of spent firecrackers and stale toffee. Red wagons. "A traveling troupe?"

Iiliana looked up. "Yes—I think you're right. Twinmoon—that is where Elric was, last we had word from him."

Caitlin left Iiliana to dispatch her message, returning to her own chambers to sit and ponder. Everything had the mark of Myrrhlock, the necromancer she had thought destroyed. She wanted to believe with all her heart that Iiliana was wrong, that Myrrhlock had been defeated. At length Caitlin rose and went to the basin of water at her washstand; looking into the surface, she sent out a silent summons with her mind for a vision of Iimogen's captor. Just as an image was forming on the water's surface, her concentration was broken by a silent, keening call, a mute, insistent crying.

Caitlin drew aside the curtain and looked into the cradle, where the goblin baby lay. Its great yellow eyes reproached her. It did not cry, but Caitlin's mind filled with its complaint as with the silent pitch of a pipe that makes a dog cuff its ears.

With a sigh, she lifted the child—if it was that—from the cradle and put it to her breast, not without guilt, for she remembered Iiliana's warning. It did not bite; she had known that it would not, even as she knew that neither milk nor beef broth would long sustain it. Abagtha's old book of incantations had proven maddeningly vague on the subject of goblins, and what there was of the short entry had been nearly obliterated by a stain. Caitlin looked down at the sucking child. It held her gaze unblinkingly, and with hands that were too large for a baby it kneaded her chest with a kittenish motion that pricked with the same sharpness.

Caitlin knew she should not name it, knew all that naming it would mean, both for it and for Bram. But quite unbidden its name rose in her mind, a cipher in wax, spinning in the water of her basin: *Grimald.* The huge yellow eyes seemed to will her to say it aloud.

"No," she said to the goblin firmly, and abruptly returned it to the cradle. It pursed its mouth in disapproval.

"And that's the closest you'll get to a howl, I suppose."

In answer, the golden eyes blinked deliberately, and the goblin curled its hands docilely over the counterpane.

Elric and the Badger had ridden into Twinmoon, sleeping in ditches, to which practice Elric attributed the strange ailment that felled the Badger their third night out.

It started with wakefulness, an inability to shut his eyes, that lasted seven nights. All night, while Elric slept, the Badger filled page after page of a notebook with strange runes, to get them out of his head. On the third night of his ailment the Badger woke Elric with a scream of terror, claiming demons on the other side of the campfire were going to spit him and roast him alive. The next morning Elric missed him, only to find him inside a hollow tree, a crown of mushrooms around his head, counting backward. It was with a sinking heart that Elric recognized in the Badger the symptoms of the same malady that had claimed the townfolk of Oncemoon.

"Hell, I'm no nursemaid," he muttered, and dealt with the problem in the simplest way he knew. He bundled the

Badger into a sack so that only his head protruded and trussed him up like a sausage. They went on down the road like that, the Badger singing silly nonsense. At last, fearing he was going more than a little crazy, too, Elric found himself joining in, adding the harmony.

That night, made sleepless by the Badger's feverish wakefulness, Elric feared he, too, had begun to hallucinate. At the edge of the campfire he saw a shadow flit, a beggar child one moment, something fetched from a tomb the next. But as soon as he wheeled to face it, there was nothing but a ragged branch tossing in the wind to mock him.

The Badger was in a calm mood, and Elric had left his arms out of the sack, his wrists in a loose hobble so he could write in the earth with a sharp stick. Over and over he wrote the same verse, "Master Donkey-Ears and Mistress Catawauler / Caught more fish than they could swaller." This did not satisfy, and the Badger rubbed it out, then chewed on the end of his stick to sharpen it. This blackened his mouth and chin so he seemed a toothless beggar, tied in a sack by an innkeeper tired of keeping him in drunkenness.

Elric was afraid to let sleep overtake him. To keep awake, he set his brain at a tease, to put the Badger's lunatic lyric to a song, biting his knuckles to stay awake. Madness, he was sure, lay in repose. In the middle of the fifth refrain, "Donkey-Ears, Donkey-Ears, Dame Catawauler's got the shears," sleep overcame his best defense, and he sank into it as a stone.

And here was madness after all, waiting for him, come this time as a girl. Elric bolted up, biting the air for fright.

"Damn you, you little witch," he said, when he saw it was Grisaudra.

The stuff of her dress shimmered; that was what had caught his eye outside the fire's circle, all ghostly. She moved, and Elric saw she wore a soldier's coat of mail, belted with a rope of flowers, borage for courage, and motherwort to ward off mischief. Grisaudra held a stoppered flask out to him; he sniffed the steam suspiciously.

"One of your potions?"

"Mint tea. It's for him, but you look as though you could use some yourself."

He could have, but Elric wouldn't have admitted it for anything. It was bad enough she'd scared him out of a nightmare, as if he were no better than a boy too small to send for eggs.

She went and kneeled by the Badger, who was too intent on his scratchings to care that she pressed a thumb in his kidney and turned his eyelid inside out. Her hand crept around his neck and up the nape, feeling his skull, reading the blind man's letters for memory.

"What are you doing?" Elric asked uneasily.

"When you left me, not all of him went with you."

Elric let out his breath, relieved it was anything so earthly as that. "Is that all you want? Well, he can't marry, but there *is* a special fund . . ."

"Not *that*, you idiot! His brain, that's what the poor devil's left behind, and I wish to hyssop I could get him out of mine."

Elric was standing beside her now, wrapped in his blanket, for the scare had chilled his blood. "I've yet to hear a word of sense come out of your mouth. How can he have left his brain behind?"

Grisaudra released her grip on the Badger's head, and he quickly began to trace letters on the ground. "When I read him to do the drops, I had to read his memory in order to get a picture of his ghost."

"Her name is Caitlin, and she's very much alive."

Grisaudra shrugged. "But a ghost, all the same. You yourself called him a haunted man. Well, something's gone awry, and I haven't been able to get his memories out of my head.

They're becoming a real nuisance, and I'm here to give them back."

A nuisance indeed; she woke that morning to find her neck and wrists sore and blistered, as if a rope or some other bonds had chafed them. The cat, formerly immured in indifference, now swarmed over her, purring, so that Grisaudra would have staked her life there were a dozen cats instead of one. And the dreams. Not unpleasant, no, to the contrary! Very pleasant, so that when she woke from them she could have wept from disappointment.

Well, it had to stop! The shirt of mail she wore held the cold and made Grisaudra toss in her sleep, to keep the dreams at bay. But it kept sleep from her just as efficiently, and in the morning the cat looked at her mistress curiously, as Grisaudra swore at the wet matches and kicked the kettle.

She had finally lit the fire and set the kettle over it when the ghost overcame her. She found herself kneeling by the Badger while he lay near death, only it was winter and she was not Grisaudra, but the ghostly beauty, Caitlin. Surely as she knew Caitlin had once saved the Badger's life, the spell-seller of the Oncemoon Marsh knew that selfsame life, or the best part of it, lay in the balance again. What's more, she knew with more certainty than she liked that the soundness of her own mind was now caught up with the Badger and his ghost.

"Damn those drops!" she'd said, setting out a bowl of water for the cat and piece of cheese to draw mice. "The old man warned me about them." Grisaudra had then set off for Twinmoon, where she had heard the madness had spread and where she knew she'd find Elric and the Badger.

"He's got the same sickness," Elric said.

"Or at least the same strain. Unless I've missed him in his swanthistle petticoat. Now, *that* must've been a sight!"

"I don't see anything to laugh about."

"Sometimes laughter's the only poultice that will draw out the poison."

"Well, mint tea certainly isn't going to purge him, I guarantee you. Look at him! I should never have taken him for that cure of yours. I'd rather he were merely mad with love than mad for madness' sake."

"Well, it's some mischief other than my drops. He was right enough in his reason, wasn't he, when you left me?"

Elric had to admit it was so.

"Then it isn't a ghost in his brain that's bothering him. It's the beast on his back."

As if on cue, the Badger suddenly began to howl in terror, beating desperately about him so that the sack toppled over, rolling perilously close to the fire in his panic. In order to protect him from his own frenzy, they had to bind the Badger in his sack once more.

A beast on his back: The thought made Elric shiver, for in his mind he could see something—shaggy, taloned, fierce—clinging to his own shoulders with a deadly grip. Whether the creature was madness in store for him or the offspring of his own fear, the red-haired knight was not willing to wager. For hadn't he slept where the Badger had and eaten of the same dishes? Elric was afraid with every passing moment that his own mind would begin to slip from reason's grasp.

In truth, however, the two had not eaten the same. At the judge's house, the husband had offered them a meal. Elric thought the bread moldy and had fed it to the dog, but the Badger had been hungry enough to dip his in the sauce and eat it anyway.

Not six hours after they had ridden off, the dog had begun to behave in the most peculiar fashion, barking and snapping at the air, chasing its tail as if demons were after it. In the morning the husband had come out to find it lying by the well house, quite dead.

By the end of the third day on the road, the old nurse, Ordella, and the baby had reached the Weirdwood, the great dark forest in the heart of Thirdmoon. It would have taken a person with an inexhaustible number of fresh horses, riding night and day at a breakneck pace, at least a week and a half to go the same distance, yet Ordella never broke into a jog that would have awakened the baby. The elf-woman knew one of the old tricks from the Elder Age, before the Necromancer had banned the elvish tongues. Half of it was a simple charm, placing feathers inside the felt of her shoes. The other half, the elder charm, Ordella's mother had called "skeining": You looked at the end of the road unfolding in front of you and imagined it as a piece of yarn. In your mind, you wound it up as fast as you could, so that it made a ball in your hand, hard and smooth as a stone.

When she had reached the Weirdwood, Ordella stopped to rest and take the feathers out of her shoes. There was no need to hurry now; this leg of the journey was nearly over. Bram slept soundly, having been dosed with some of the stonecrop cordial Iiliana kept to treat her occasional insomnia, and Ordella had tied a cat's whisker about the child's left toe, an elvish remedy, just to be sure.

When she was rested, Ordella put her shoes back on and stood up. Standing in the middle of a small clearing in the thick growth of trees, she sniffed loudly, sounding for all the world like a pig rooting for acorns. Evidently she smelled what she was seeking, for she gave out a satisfied grunt and set the baby down at the roots of an ancient oak. Set in the trunk and grown over with moss was a red door. Below it, skillfully covered over so no human eyes could detect it, was a second, smaller door that came only to Ordella's knees. She knelt down and drew a silver key from one pocket, slipping it into the lock. Ordella did not know as she put her shoulder to the task that another old woman had once carried a baby to this very oak or that the other baby had grown into the mother of this one. Ordella knew not and cared not, just muttered a mild curse at the rusty hinges.

Inside the oak it was black as a chimney sweep's fingernails and smelled of a feather pillow that had been left out in the rain. Ordella did not light a lamp or kindle a fire but carried Bram straight down a winding stair, past a small nut-cellar, to a trapdoor deep among the roots of the old oak tree. The elf-woman drew a key from around her neck, and it turned in the lock smooth as butter. When she opened the trapdoor, the damp, earthen passage was flooded with a warm orange glow. At this, Bram awoke and began to whimper.

As well he might, or might any human child waking hungry, far from his mother, to find himself on the back stoop of the Otherworld.

How Many Ravens?

*T*illie shivered where she slept, though it was warmer in the tent than it had been in the wagon. She was dreaming of the day she had walked out of the house to feed the geese only to find them all dead, the smallest gosling floating in the horses' watering trough.

She dreamed of her mother in the throes of the fever, screaming in terror that the walls of the bedchamber were wolves' jaws, snarling and snapping. Tillie could hardly believe the madwoman in the bed was her mother. Her mother, who used to sit by the fire, stitching a golden vine and leaves all around a pair of dancing slippers, while Tillie read aloud. Now she struck the spoon from Tillie's hand, seeing maggots in the bowl instead of gruel.

The dream—which was a memory also—always ended the same way. The fever seemed to break: Her mother sat up and asked for her needle and thread. Weeping with glad relief, Tillie brought them, and while her mother began to embroider the felt of the slipper, the dream-Tillie would lay her head on the blanket by her mother's knee and sleep for the first time in days.

In the dream, she woke to find her mother still stitching, the whole slipper by now completely encrusted with thread, so thick with a pattern in gold and scarlet that none of the slipper underneath could be seen. And her mother had not stopped with the slipper. When that was done, she had continued the pattern onto the blanket, sewing her night-shirt fast to the bed sheet. All the same pattern, in red and gold, a pattern of wolves' gullets, opened wide.

Tillie woke with a muffled scream. By the fire the Necromancer looked up from the maze of glasswork, where he was distilling a purplish essence. At his feet, like a pet greyhound, slept Iimogen. At her neck a hollow glass bell gave a purple glint.

"You have had another nightmare," Myrrhlock said mildly. As he spoke, he drew off some of the purplish liquid into a glass pipe. Removing his thumb from the end of the tube, he let the liquid fall into a small silver-and-crystal cordial glass.

"Yes, a nightmare," Tillie answered. The firelight on the glasswork, the Necromancer's goblinstone skullcap, the way Iimogen lay in some enchantment—all this might be some strange dream, too.

For Tillie was remembering a music she had heard, music she had at first thought was the kettle singing or her mother's feverish humming, high and melodic, the way golden stitching would sound if it were given a voice in music, a bright and twining thread of sound.

Then Tillie remembered the strange figure with a flute, wearing a cloak lined with silk in a pattern of poppies, leading the children out of the town, a goose leading goslings, a fox leading geese.

"You—" Tillie started to raise herself from the pallet to pull the twigs of swanthistle from her hair.

But the Necromancer's hand was already on the back of her neck, the glass pressed against her teeth like a steel bit, and she must drink the stuff down. In a minute, she was curled at the Necromancer's feet with Iimogen, her eyes blinking as the drops fell through the glass apparatus, collecting in the wide-bellied flask like liquid amethyst.

Myrrhlock's eye was caught by something in the corner. It was a hollow glass ball.

Ah, he thought, *so that explains it.* Myrrhlock picked up the ball and refastened it around Tillie's neck.

Caitlin could not sleep. She had drunk a cup of wine, but it had left her even more wakeful, playing game after game of geese-and-foxes until Iiliana pushed the board away, protesting that she would drop from weariness. After Iiliana went off to bed, Caitlin played a few more games against herself. The clock showed its pinched, small-morning-hour face; the trees tossed and turned outside her window; somewhere, far off, the sea snored.

Caitlin picked up and handled the small vial of purple stuff by her bedside, the ergot Iiliana had dosed her with to ease the pain of her labor with Bram. "Heaven knows the wine's not working," she muttered to herself. Not bothering to hunt for a spoon, Caitlin filled the hollow stopper with a thimble's measure and tossed it down like brandy.

The glass salamander shone softly on the stand next to the vial. Caitlin had fallen into the habit of petting it, rubbing her thumb along the curve of its coiled head and tail. She picked it up now and immediately felt soothed. Though the seer's glass had shown her nothing since the day on the rocks, Caitlin could not help silently beseeching it to show her Bram. She squeezed the glass tightly.

With a cry, Caitlin flung the salamander to the floor. She could have sworn it had bitten her, if she hadn't known well the delirium brought on by sleeplessness. As she bent to pick it up, Caitlin again admired the skill of the ancient glassmaker; true to life, the salamander's belly was white and the legs better modeled than she remembered them. You would swear the thing was real.

The ergot was having no better success than the wine. Caitlin paused in her prowling to peek into Grimald's cradle. The changeling was sleepless, too, or else its keener hearing had perceived Caitlin's light tread on the carpet as she paced. It gave a silent whimper and cry, and she knew it was hungry. Caitlin lifted the changeling from the cradle and walked the floor with it.

"The kitchen's closed, my little goblin. Besides, you've had two bowls of beef broth for your dinner. At that rate, you'll be needing a rowboat for a cradle before long."

Grimald *was* growing. It was his mind, his silent, insistent voice that was getting stronger every day. *Feed me,* he demanded. *Name me. I am Grimald. I am yours, as you are mine.*

Well, it has teeth, she thought. Perhaps it will let me sleep if I give it some solid food. She kept a secret store of macaroons in the bottom drawer of her nightstand. At the first crinkling of the paper, Grimald opened his eyes. As Grimald bit into the first one, he gave a grunt of pleasure, like a baby pig, and made Caitlin laugh. The golden eyes glowed, the small pointed tongue ran around the wide goblin mouth. The macaroon was gone, and the goblin fell asleep in her arms. Caitlin lay down on the bed. It was nearly dawn. With her eyes closed, but for the light pricking of the goblin nails, it was almost possible to believe it was Bram asleep at her breast.

"Go to sleep, Grimald," Caitlin murmured as she drifted off to sleep.

On the nightstand the glass salamander had uncurled. One by one it slowly worked free its legs, uncoiling from its long sleep. As Caitlin spoke the goblin's name aloud, the salamander opened its eyes.

The passage down which Ordella carried her stolen baby

was covered with carpets of otherworldly workmanship and walls hung with tapestries surpassing human skill. The orange glow was cast not by rough torches but by lamps fueled with underground ethers. From time to time the elf-woman would pass a spot along the passage that showed signs of recent repair, where human trespassers—miners, eloping lovers, prisoners escaping their cells—had dug through into the Otherworld. On the human side of the wall the searchers would not know what to make of the wadded remains of torn clothing and a few mementos, like the pellets an owl makes out of the mice on which it dines. The search party would return to the light and air to report that the search had come to an unhappy end.

The missing were not dead, but neither were they wholly living. On the otherworld side of the wall the fugitives were taken in as half-castes, able to dimly recall the human world but never to return to it. Oddly, it was these interlopers who made the most beautiful tapestries, more highly prized than anything of elvish hands.

Some humans, however, could freely pass from the one world to the other. These were seers, oracles born with one blue eye and one green, who could see into the future at will. Caitlin was one such otherworld daughter, and it was for this reason that Ordella had been dispatched to fetch away her firstborn son. Bram's name, "little raven," was itself a charm to guarantee the plot's success, for the raven was the messenger of the Otherworld. For how was a group of such birds known but as *an unkindness of ravens?* When a number were sighted roosting in a leafless tree, shrewd folk knew a door to the Otherworld, and its attendant dangers, could not be far away.

Ordella did not pause either to admire the tapestries or to examine the patched portions of the walls. Both were well-known to her, and she hurried Bram past them without a thought either for the fate of the weavers or that of the trespassers. Ordella was in a hurry; babies were the most resilient, yet the most vulnerable, of the human interlopers in the Otherworld. Bram must be brought quickly to the court and given mole's milk boiled with elves' rosemary, which unlike its earthly cousin was the herb of forgetfulness, not remembrance. This brew was effective in making human children forget their mothers, and without it they quickly pined away. As soon as he woke from his drugged slumber, Bram would be dosed and the drops would be put in his eyes to accustom them to otherworld light. It had once been the fashion to dye the human changeling's eyes goblin yellow, but this only turned blue and green eyes a murky amber, and the practice had all but fallen out of favor.

The corridor spiraled downward. The farther Ordella went into the caverns the brighter the light became, until at last the long corridor emptied into a large chamber. Here all the tapestries were wrought in silver, the work of a young woman who had thought to elope with her beloved, only to wake and find herself in the Otherworld. The light came from hundreds of translucent crystal lamps, lit with a different gas that perfumed the chamber and burned with a cooler, more silvery light. One whole wall was covered in a white flowering vine, the underground cultivation of flowers being one of the foremost elven arts. Next to the flowers, on a silver chaise fashioned in the shape of a grasshopper, reclined the elf queen, arranging blossoms in a vessel of ether. Ylfcwen was molting, and her new set of wings lay wetly across her back. The process was not painful, but the tedium of immobility to prevent tearing her wings had left the elf queen lethargic and more than a little peeved.

Ordella surrendered Bram to the nurses, who quickly gathered round. As they were about to give the baby the tonic of forgetfulness, Ylfcwen raised her hand.

"No, don't. Oh, put the drops in his eyes, all right, but don't give him any milk."

"Madam, the day-child will pine away if we do not."

The elf queen shrugged, as much to dry her wings a little

as to express her indifference. "Day-child, night-child, he could be a four-in-the-afternoon child and you'd still have to set aside the mole's milk. There has been a change in plans. Drusian would have the child."

Yet Ylfcwen pushed the flowers away and tipped her head to one side. "But do set him by me, just for a bit."

Iiliana's stonecrop cordial had worn off, and Bram looked around him, his gaze held by the colored paper orbs of fireflies that lent more decoration than light. But he quickly gave his attention to the pretty lavender blood to be seen flowing beneath Ylfcwen's transparent skin, her iridescent wings and opal eyes without a dark center. The baby remembered his mother and would have cried for Caitlin except for the cat's whisker around his left great toe.

"Poor thing!" Ylfcwen cried, and bent forward to kiss his brow. "You look like you're going to explode from not crying." The elf queen looked up in sudden alarm. "He can't really explode, can he?"

"No, madam, though madam might tickle him, so as to vent him a little." Ylfcwen picked Bram up, fascinated by his smell of mingled sugar and salt, talc and milk and wet diaper, with a hint of that woody-musky human smell so unlike the cooling-jasmine-tea smell of an elf baby or the hot-sealing-wax-and-burnt-paper smell of a goblin.

The cat's whisker had loosened and fallen off, and Bram began to whimper with hunger, then cry with it in earnest.

Ylfcwen nearly dropped him. "What's that?"

"He's hungry, madam. Since he's not to have the mole's milk, perhaps madam would like to give him a little nectar."

Ylfcwen breathed in Bram's smell, narrowing her opal eyes. "Yes. Let's give the day-child some nectar."

Caitlin woke from a deep sleep, not at all surprised to find the glass salamander on her pillow. She was surprised that it now seemed to be alive, but perhaps not so surprised as she should have been, and was only mildly astonished to find that it could speak.

"My name," the salamander explained, "is obscure and nearly unpronounceable by human tongues. So it will suffice if you call me Newt."

Caitlin raised herself up on one elbow. "But why should I need to call you anything? This is a dream, and you're nothing more than a pretty piece of glass that I happened to look at as I was falling off to sleep."

"Oh? You think I'm part of your dream, do you? Go to the window, then, and have a look."

Caitlin got up and went to the window. The brilliant sunshine blinded her at first, but as soon as her eyes adjusted she could see Iiliana walking around the garden, bouncing the goblin baby in her arms to amuse it. The fly that buzzed in her ear, the smell of the flowering vine, the heat of the sun all conspired to convince her.

So I am awake, Caitlin thought.

"Just so," said Newt.

"Don't be rude," she said, alarmed that a glass gewgaw could read her thoughts.

"It's all right," said the salamander, *"you can read mine, too.* Let me up on your shoulder, though, and I'll speak in your ear."

Caitlin lifted him gently to her shoulder, and the salamander twined his feet in her hair to hold on.

"When I was little," Caitlin said, "I used to play with lizards, dried ones, from Abagtha's jars." Her old guardian had kept a strange pantry full of such things for brewing potions and other mischiefs.

"There was a book, too," said Newt.

"Yes . . . her book of incantations. It's here in the palace, in Iiliana's chambers. She had it fetched here from the Weird-wood with some other things after I came, while I was with the seals." Iiliana had brought the book to her room to restore, taking to it with soft brushes and a magnifying glass when her other duties vexed her.

Caitlin went to the sill and looked out. Iiliana was still in the garden, picking feathers out of the birdbath; she had left the goblin baby on the arbor seat, and a raven had flown down to perch by Grimald's feet.

"Let's go find it." For Caitlin suddenly felt an overwhelming urge to see Abagtha's book of incantations, and her training as a seer had taught her to respect her urges. She was not entirely sure whether she was in the middle of a vision or just a very odd dream, but the worst thing that could happen, she supposed, was that she would be caught sleepwalking. "I don't think Iiliana's taken it to the library yet. Let's have a look in her chamber."

As she walked along the gallery that opened on the seafront, no one seemed to notice Caitlin or the salamander perched on her shoulder. They slipped unseen into Iiliana's chamber. The book of incantations lay under a glass dome borrowed from the kitchen, meant to cover cheese. Caitlin removed the dome and set it on the floor beside Iiliana's work table. It was a heavy tome on a carved wooden stand, three ribbons marking its places, one blue, one silver, one green. The runes were thick and tangled like the thorny hedge around an abandoned castle, the gilt of the miniature paintings dulled by dust and worn by the bookworm's tooth.

The queen of Chameol had been restoring the entry on dreams. The illustration in the margin showed a fair young man with golden hair asleep under a tree in which there roosted three ravens. The young man's horse could be seen in the distance, where it had wandered off to gorge on windfall apples.

"Oh!" Caitlin jumped, so that Newt had to tighten his grip on her shoulder. "Now there are four ravens."

"Five," said Newt.

Something very strange was happening to the book. Before Caitlin's eyes another raven joined the other five, and soon there were seven. Though the window to Iiliana's chamber was closed, the pages of the book began to turn over rapidly, as if blown by a strong wind. There were no runes anymore, only a swarming mass of brilliant color, color that overran the page, filled the room with vines and birds and apes riding donkeys, making such a racket Caitlin expected all the palace to break down the door any minute.

"Quickly," said Newt. "The door."

And there *was* a door, right in the spot where a moment ago had stood Iiliana's washstand. What's more, it was a red door, very like the one in the ancient oak where she had lived with Abagtha so long ago. Indeed, the walls of the room had grown rough and woody like bark, the wallpaper peeling off in green leaves.

Caitlin stepped forward and bent to open the small red door, and in a moment she had stepped through it into the Otherworld.

Ghosts Again

*I*n the dream, Grisaudra was fifteen again. She let herself into her parents' cottage with the key that hung around her neck. The silence got up to greet her. The dogs did not run out barking "Grr-g'morrrow!" Her sisters were not fighting over whose turn it was to feed the pigs. She listened, but there was no hushed murmur of rushes as her mother sat by the fire, making baskets.

She went into the yard. The sight made Grisaudra sadder than the fact that there had been no one home to greet her. The yard was full of mud and soot from the forge, blackened parings, broken dishes, and empty bottles. Her father's blacksmith's tools were gone. So were the horses.

"Father?"

A lone goose stuck its neck out from under the cow shed. Grisaudra recognized it as the goose that laid no golden eggs: it laid no eggs at all. The family had taken everything of use with them. Even the weather vane, the girl could imagine her mother saying, could be sold for shoes. It was perfectly good brass.

Then the girl noticed a marker not quite covered over with mud and soot, in one corner of the yard.

REMEMBER GRISAUDRA
LOST IN THE BATTLE FOR TENTHMOON
YEAR OF THE PENTACLE
NINE HUNDRED TWENTY-FIVE

Grisaudra woke choked with the terror and furious despair she had felt those fifteen years ago, returning from the wars to find her family had moved on, giving her up for dead. Still wearing her vest of chain mail, she had taken the goose and wandered on, earning her bread for a while with a troupe of traveling players until at last she reached the marshes of Oncemoon, where the old hermit had taken her in and taught her the secrets of the plants of marsh and meadow. No draught he could concoct, however, had been able to rid Grisaudra of her memories. She would rather relive the battles, hear again the sword blade singing silver toward her face, than relive that homecoming.

Now Grisaudra raised herself on one elbow and felt beneath her pallet for a vial. Catmint and juniper, more powerful than brandy, a drug if taken in a prudent dose, a poison if taken immoderately. Grisaudra allowed herself the smallest of swallows; when it was gone, who knew when she could manage to brew more? She corked and capped the vial and returned it to its hiding place. Soon she had drifted off, amnesiac at least until day should break.

Elric had seen her. At worst, he brooded, she is a cold-blooded poisoner, at best, an unreliable addict. He resolved to determine the contents of the vial at the first opportunity.

The Badger woke from his madness. Elric arose to find him sitting by the fire, his hand shaking as if from age or drunkenness as he raised a cup of tea to his lips.

"You're with us, then . . . ?"

The Badger nodded cautiously, as if not sure himself. "It seems I'm safely back." He had washed the sweat and stink away in the stream; his gold hair was dark with water, raked back from his face, and his clothes lay scattered over the hedges. He wore Elric's other trousers and his own leather vest.

Elric quizzed the Badger lightly, without seeming to, ascertaining that the Badger knew his own name as well as

Elric's, remembered that he was a knight of Chameol, and recalled visiting Grisaudra's hut. It seemed the fever had not boiled his brain dry.

Yet the Badger himself seemed troubled. "Don't think me an ass," he said suddenly. "It's just that I'm still coming out of a murk. But what is this, and why am I wearing it?"

And he held out the wrist that was cinched with a braided ebony circlet of Caitlin's hair. Elric felt his heart sink, a stone in a well. He wet his lips before he could bring himself to a second examination.

"You have no memory of the bracelet?"

"None."

"Does the name Asaph mean anything to you?"

"Of course! He's the monk who raised me and a knight like you and me."

"Iiliana?"

"Queen of Chameol and your sister."

"Abagtha?"

The Badger frowned. "Something—but I don't—is it her bracelet, then?"

"No. How about the name Cassandra? Calliope? Cressie?"

The Badger only shook his head. "No, not a thing." His face, furrowed in concentration, went suddenly smooth with panic. "Please . . . Tell me—is she my sister?"

"No. Just a friend you knew, once." Elric was afraid to tell him more and frighten the Badger from any memory he might yet retain. To tell a man he had forgotten the woman he loved . . .

"But that's what you asked me to do, make him forget," Grisaudra pointed out. As soon as she was awake, Elric had pulled her aside to acquaint her with this most recent development in their patient.

"But not completely! To him, it would be like losing an eye—or a leg," he amended hastily, suddenly remembering Grisaudra's own eye. "By satisfying his heart's desire, you were to cool his passion enough for him to move about in the world again, for him to sleep in peace."

"And so I did. It was the fever did this to him." Grisaudra jerked her head in the direction where the Badger was saddling the horses.

Elric shook his head. "It's as though someone had taken a pair of shears and snipped out the part of his memory with her in it."

What was this woman the Badger could not remember? A tall creature, sleek and supple as a cat, her face the blue milk of marble in moonlight, set with mismatched seer's eyes. Her hair was a cascade of inky silk, grown out from the shearing it had been given by an eel-seller's knife, sold in barter for a map. He had forgotten the throat and wrists it had been impossible for him to kiss without remembering the bells placed there by the fearful and superstitious.

The Badger had forgotten all this, forgotten the day they met, when she had bitten and kicked him, forgotten how slowly, slowly her shrugs and sullen stares had turned to more solemn gazes and even smiles. He did not remember the morning he had first awakened to find her in his arms, no longer reluctant in any way, holding back nothing of herself. The memory of that kiss was gone as surely as if the kiss itself had never been. Now it lay, curled tight as an acorn, waiting within the halves of its woody locket, waiting buried beneath great frozen drifts of forgetfulness.

Poor Grisaudra remembered all this and more. Elric, out of cruelty or a disinclination to intervene, had said nothing when the Badger had offered Grisaudra a seat before him on the piebald Motley. So she had to ride with the Badger's arms circled round her holding the reins, like a country bride. And how could she object? If he couldn't remember

Caitlin, the Badger couldn't be expected to believe in the ghost of her memory.

But it was her own memory of a warm, corporeal embrace that played itself over and over again in her mind. The welt where she had hit her head had subsided and was no longer tender, but Grisaudra's heart—so long hardened against any siege—was beginning to feel tender for the first time in years.

Darting glances at the conjurer from where he rode a few paces to the side, Elric began to regret having ever visited the hut in the middle of the marsh. We would all have been better off, he thought, if I had simply let him wrap his head in cheesecloth. As it was, the red-haired knight was afraid he would soon have a lovesick herbwoman on his hands as well as an amnesiac knight. If he didn't already.

Newt guided Caitlin along the corridor, following in Ordella's footsteps. The salamander's eyes gleamed, and he tightened his grip on Caitlin's shoulder.

"It might be best *not* to walk in the front door."

"Very well. We'll go in the back way." Caitlin pulled aside the tapestries that lined the hallway until she found one that hid a door. The knob turned in her hand, and the door opened silently on elven hinges.

They were clearly in a nursery. Caitlin's heart beat wildly as she crept up to the first cradle, where a transparent globe of fireflies hung to amuse the infant. But when she drew the gauzy curtain aside, a yellow goblin stare met her eyes.

"There is no need to look in the other cradles," Newt told her. "This is where they keep the changelings until they are ready to make the exchange."

But Caitlin had known, though her heart rose up against the knowing, that Bram was not in any of the cradles. She would have known in a minute, would have smelled his damp, dark hair and the radiating sweetness from under his chin and the creases of his plump knees, the faint waxiness of the sleepy-sticks in his eyes. There had only been a wet-matches-and-burnt-sugar smell of goblin, which the elves disguised under a liberal sprinkling of crushed orange blossom and clove water.

And before she could turn away in disappointment, Caitlin was assailed by the memory of another smell, of leather and clean brass and wood smoke, the smell of the Badger's riding jacket. For the first time since Bram had vanished, Caitlin broke down and wept, for Bram had been her comfort for that other loss. Now she felt keenly the twin bereavement, and her arms ached for Bram and the Badger both.

Suddenly, the salamander was biting her ear, and Caitlin felt a quickly spreading numbness, and with it a feeling of well-being, as if Newt had untied the twisted knot of her heart. She reached up to remove the creature from her ear, rubbing it under the chin in silent gratitude.

There was a light gasp in the room, and they turned to see Ylfcwen in the doorway, summoned by the novel sound of a human woman weeping. Elves only threw tantrums, and the closest goblins got to crying was a case of the hiccoughs.

Ylfcwen quickly regained her composure. "I warrant you've come about the baby."

"My son," Caitlin said. "Yes, that's my business with you."

Ylfcwen came up to Caitlin and looked her over at nearer scrutiny. The elf queen might have felt at a disadvantage, wearing pajamas and having her wings rolled in a silk-and-parchment nightcase, but the idea that she should ever feel ill at ease had never occurred to her and it did not do so now. The fact that the pajamas were embroidered with dragonflies' wings only made the queen look more otherworldly.

"Come to my chambers, and we will talk about this—bram—of yours."

Ylfcwen jingled slightly as she moved, from the small silver bells on her ankles, which made her heavier than air and enabled her to walk. Although there were chambers with ceilings high enough to allow flight, flying was undertaken only to keep one's wings fit and for certain arcane ceremonies. Only if she was having difficulty sleeping did the elf queen slip off her anklets and let herself drift to the ceiling to drowse in the clouds of incense amidst the golden murmuring of fireflies.

The gardeners had trained wood violets and lily of the valley to grow along the walls of Ylfcwen's chambers, so that the effect in the high-ceilinged room was of having fallen into a steep pit lined with flowers. Ylfcwen's pet mole slept on the foot of the silken bed. A small table was littered with a great many finely wrought silver instruments used in the care of the queen's wings.

Ylfcwen scooped up the mole and sat where it had been dozing, indicating with a gesture that Caitlin should be seated herself.

Caitlin shook her head. "I would rather you took me to see Bram."

Ylfcwen sighed and struck a silver tuning fork on the end of the bedpost. An elf servant appeared with a flask of amber nectar. Newt murmured in Caitlin's ear, "It might be better for your purposes if you did nothing to offend. Sit and drink with her, and perhaps she will tell you what you want to know."

And perhaps not.

Newt bit the lobe of Caitlin's ear softly, and this time it stung instead of soothed. *Offend her, and it's* certainly *not,* the salamander replied silently.

Ylfcwen held out a silver-and-crystal cup of the liquid. To

Caitlin's surprise, it was quite cold and went down aromatic and slightly bitter. Suddenly she felt a need to sit. Ylfcwen refilled Caitlin's glass and then her own. When she had emptied her second glass, the elf queen slipped the bells from her feet, and the earthbound liquor allowed her to lie on the bed without the help of weights. This was her way of showing her earthly visitor she was accepted as an equal.

Ylfcwen's thoughts were hidden behind the veil of her moonstone eyes, those eyes without a dark center. The elf queen regarded Caitlin with sleepy curiosity before she finally spoke.

"The code is quite clear on the matter: The firstborn child of an Otherworld daughter must be named within three days and with a name of the earth only, names of fire and water carrying some risk and names of air being the most dangerous of all. You waited three *weeks* and then you named him Bram, after a bird of the air, and an Otherworld bird at that. You might as well have put him out the door for the dairyman while you were at it."

"Come, come." It was only with effort that Caitlin kept her voice level. "It was your servant-woman, Ordella, who planted that name in the jar. And she, probably, who put a little something in my tea in the morning to muddle my brain a bit and keep me from making up my mind."

Ylfcwen frowned and tugged at the laces of her nightcase. She shrugged her wings out, snapped them open and shut a few times, and began to work at the iridescent scales with a silver tool a little like a nutpick. "She might have and she might not. Those weren't my instructions to her, in any case. She was told to watch carefully, and if the conditions of the code were met, to bring the bram back with her."

Caitlin swirled the bitter amber stuff around in the bottom of her glass. "What does your code have to say about my getting him back?"

"Well, usually you would have to fill out a petition and

bribe me for a while with gifts and then perhaps serve a year or two as my personal supplicant. But I am afraid this is not a usual case."

Caitlin stood up, her heart leaping like a hare. "Why, what have you done with him? Where is he? You must tell me!"

Ylfcwen set down the nutpick and picked up a small silver file. "Don't upset yourself so. Think of my best rootwine, wasted on a case of nervous agitation! The bram is quite safe."

"Then let me *see* him."

"I'm afraid that is no longer possible. You see, he has been taken to Drusian."

"Taken where?"

"Oh, not where! Who! To Drusian—to the Master of Sleep and Desire."

Folderol's Band

Since the defeat of the Pentaclists and the routing of the monks from the temples, the thirteen kingdoms had fallen into disarray. As queen of Chameol, Iiliana faced a daunting task: to convince her subjects that Chameol was more than the shroud of mystery and legend that had for centuries surrounded it. The wild tales of an enchanted isle had long been Chameol's shield and disguise; now they threatened to usurp its very power. Iiliana found it hard to convince thirteen feuding kings to bow to the rule of a mysterious island ruled by hermit women with unpronounceable names, where the arts of the sword were not merely uncultivated but shunned. Iiliana spent much of her time dispatching knights to snuff out kindling rebellions and ambassadors to soothe the tempers of kings. The age of darkness was over, but it would take time before the thirteen splintered kingdoms emerged united into an age of light.

When the belltowers of the temples had toppled, the old tenets of the Pentacle had toppled with them—the bans on magic and free-lance sorcery not the least among them. Competition was fierce, and where aspiring sorcerors and apothecaries had neither the talent nor the guile to make a living, they soon gave their energies over to another, more lucrative calling. Roving bands of highwaymen and deserters were joined on the roads by itinerant troupes of acrobats and palm readers, and there was often more to liken them to the robbers than to distinguish them.

Chief among these bands, whether reckoned by quantity (sheer numbers of tent pegs, juggler's bats, flea-bitten animals, and more flea-bitten trainers) or quality (the spectacular absurdity of its freaks, the unsurpassed ineptitude of its jugglers, the sheer moral decrepitude of its owner) was the ragtag ensemble that answered to the bark of an old sailor and hired sword named Folderol.

For a while, the ranks had thinned; the talking pig had eaten some bad chestnuts and died, the tumbling dwarves had defected to a rival troupe for better wages, and his star attraction, the leopard-woman, had retired to join her sister-in-law in a dressmaking enterprise. But none of these setbacks had stopped Folderol for very long. He sat in his tent, his gouty foot raised on a folding footstool, counting the evening's receipts. Not bad, he thought, and better for that new boy. A strange little creature, hair like milkweed, so quiet you'd think he was mute, too tiny even to carry the chestnut roaster through the throng. But he could still work the crowd; the box in Folderol's lap showed the booty: an assortment of gold coins, two watches, four snuffboxes, and a small, gilt-over-silver hearing trumpet. Folderol tweaked his grizzled calico whiskers pensively, weighing the benefits to his accounts book of keeping the boy on against his own unease around Nix's partner.

This was Ulfra, a young woman in an old soldier's uniform and a gilt-and-paste crown, first seen driving seven wolves before her along the road, Nix perched on the shoulders of the largest, a silver giant that must have been three-quarters Direwolf. Ulfra's slight, slope-shouldered stance and bent knees, like those of a dog walking on its hind legs, and the careful way she had to wrap consonants around the howl that rode through the middle of her speech made Folderol think Ulfra must be at least a quarter Direwolf herself.

With short barks and growls Ulfra had put the pack through their paces, getting them to walk first on their hind legs, then on their front ones. They would run in a ring within a ring, Nix leaping from wolf to wolf as though they were stepping-stones. As a finale, Ulfra took tidbits of meat between her lips, and the wolves put their paws on her shoulders to kiss her without harming her at all.

This act had since been greatly refined and expanded to include the wolves singing in rounds, finishing with a pantomime of Ulfra and the largest wolf as a wife and husband at breakfast, ending with the juggling of goose eggs. SEE ULFRA THE WOLF-GIRL, the sign outside the tent read. RAISED BY DIREWOLVES AND BROUGHT TO THE COURT OF THE KING. NO WHIPS, NO SWORDS, HER FEMININE CHARMS HER ONLY PROTECTION. WITH NIX, THE ALBINO DEAF-MUTE, WHO HAS NOT THE SPEECH OF MEN BUT CAN SING WITH THE WOLVES. The sign did not begin to hint at the sound the wolves made, voices raised in eerie song, and rising through them the boy's soprano, pure and clear as melted ice. There was nothing sad about the wolves, the way there was about the dancing bears in their muzzles or the old toothless lion or the swaybacked horse wheezing beneath the burden of the overweight acrobat. Rather, there was the feeling as you watched Ulfra and her wolves that the whole act was a pantomime, a jest at the expense of the human onlookers. Sitting back on their haunches, panting through toothy grins, the wolves seemed hugely amused at their audience.

Ulfra herself had prospered. She and Nix shared a tent with their wolves, and when she was not performing, Ulfra could be found there, reclining on a couch of sleeping wolves, enjoying a meal of very rare meat from Nix's fingers or a pipe of clove. She treated the fledgling daredevil rider and veteran pickpocket as if he were a cub of hers, cuffing his ear if he did something tiresome, pinning him still with an elbow while she licked his face and hair. No human words were ever uttered in that tent, Nix and Ulfra finding it more convenient to converse in growls and low yelps, though you did hear Nix singing in that voice of melting mountain ice, singing of the wind in the wood and the deeds of old wolf warriors.

Folderol turned all this over in his mind as if it were a rich matron's jeweled pillbox that had gotten mixed in with the day's take of copper coins. As uneasy as Ulfra made him, the wolf-girl had been good for Folderol's wallet. Plucking a silver whisker from his beard and feeling magnanimous, the old rogue resolved to buy Ulfra a roast lamb in the next large town and some caramels for Nix.

He might have pulled more of his beard out than that had Folderol known Nix was skimming a fifth of the gate from the coin box nightly. Folderol might have ended up completely clean-chinned had he suspected that Ulfra's crown was not gilt and paste at all but gold, and gold with emeralds and rubies at that.

Grisaudra might have been more grateful to have someone else's dreams to dream to keep her from her own nightmares. There were any number of things she could have dreamed about to keep her from a good night's rest: the night on the battlefield, for instance, that the young soldier she adored had discovered that she was not a boy and had joined with the others in tossing the bundle of her clothes over her head, and had broken her shield, so that when the sword had come singing down there had been no way to protect herself. Or she might have dreamed again of the way the old Oncemoon wizard had died, having said too lightly a forbidden spell to call forth the shadows.

Grisaudra hardly minded riding on Motley and having to bear hours on end trapped within the circle of the reins and the Badger's arms. She found it soothing, for despite Elric's disapproval and his dire, cryptic remarks about all being lost over honey and a wasp, the Badger liked to sing softly as they rode. He had a sweet tenor and sang funny riddle songs, silly ones with endless verses, so that before she knew it they were finding a place to camp for the night. It was then Grisaudra began to mind, watching the Badger currycomb the horses, rubbing Motley's stiff knee, holding an apple in his teeth for the grey mare, Maud. *That* was a trial, watching him bend to clean the horses' shoes of stones from the road. It almost made her grateful for Elric's bickering about her inability to cook.

"Well, what do you want, when you won't let me add any herbs to the pot?"

"What, and wake up to find the soup's changed us into frogs? No thank you!" And he took the potato away and peeled it himself. Grisaudra seethed and in her mind brewed a tea for Elric of monkshood, which takes men's speech away, and wintersweet, to give him an exquisite pain.

So she should have been grateful to dream so pleasantly of the Badger's eyes gazing at her as if they saw something beautiful, his arms slipping around her, then under her, lifting her clear of the floor, clear of the earth.

Grisaudra should have been grateful. But she wasn't, not even a little bit.

A pigeon had come from Chameol, bidding Elric to follow a troupe of acrobats traveling in red wagons. The knights and their reluctant damsel headed west, following the harvest to the sea. Crafty rovers, too, would follow the harvest to villages where fattened flocks and ripening fields had filled many a pocket with coins that burned like coals.

Their disguises were at the ready, their pretenses well rehearsed. Elric was to be a juggler, Grisaudra a fortune-teller, the Badger an acrobatic rider.

Grisaudra could sew as well as she could cook, which is

to say not well at all. Though Elric knew this, he made Grisaudra fit the Badger's tight tunic.

"It's too tight!" the Badger protested.

"It can't be—look," Grisaudra said, seizing a fold of loose fabric in her hand and tugging on it.

"Not there—*here*," the Badger said, and pulled at the leotard where it cut him in the crotch.

Grisaudra, who seemed incapable of it, blushed, although it might have been in fury at Elric, who sat across the fire, laughing. The Badger's fragile sense of dignity collapsed, and nothing they could say would make him consent to so much as a sequin adorning his costume.

Elric insisted on supervising the construction of Grisaudra's disguise himself. He found an owl's nest and fashioned for the conjurer a cap of twigs and feathers, fitting close around her skull, curling around her ears, and coming to a peak in the middle of her forehead. To the tunic of chain mail Elric tied a dozen strange charms: dice in a net bag; a mouse skin complete with ears and tail; four tiny dolls tied from horsehair; half a rusty scissors; the blue-and-white handle of a broken cup; the lens from a spyglass; the joker from a pack of cards; and a child's green glove they had spotted lying in the road.

Grisaudra would not let him tie on the last charm, a twig of bittersweet. He argued that the red berries and yellow blossoms set off the green of the glove nicely.

"You'll spoil the scheme."

"And you'll spoil things you haven't dreamed of, meddling with herbs you've no inkling about."

"Why—what's bittersweet signify?"

She wouldn't answer, only turned to admire her cap of owl's feathers in the Badger's shaving glass. Turned half from him, Grisaudra showed to Elric the side of her face with the good eye and the unscarred cheek, so that as she turned and preened for her reflection, you might have thought her a young girl, too young for more serious games, intent on a game of dress up.

It was the Badger who pointed out the significance of the charms.

"Think—a playing card, dice, a child's glove—all the leavings of a carnival, the sweepings revelers leave behind them at a fair. We're on the heels of our acrobats, you may rely on it."

And it was so. The sun was going down, and they were standing at the top of a hill where the road began its descent into a town, when Grisaudra stretched out a hand and showed them the low, crouching shapes of the tents and the glimmer of campfires. Elric held the lens of the spyglass to his eye and squinted, then pronounced that the wagons were red indeed.

The flap of the largest tent was lifted at their whistle by the shortest, widest man they had ever seen, as if a giant had been compressed by great force into a pudding mold. This burly figure had been giving Folderol his nightly massage, and the trouper sat up on his cot, pink from his bath and wearing a towel.

Folderol nodded the strongman his leave to go. "Not hiring," was all he said to his guests, but he looked them up and down with interest anyway. When he learned their specialties, Folderol had to work hard to give a convincing display of indifference. His own daredevil rider wanted sacking; he had never quite recovered from a bad fall, and after the accident he became ever more partial to gin. Folderol had been trying to secure a reliable fortune-teller for years, and this girl looked the genuine article. Now, if he could only convince the juggler to go on in an apron and cap as the bearded dutchess. Folderol had jugglers coming out of his ears, but such an attraction as the leopard-woman had been would make him rich as a king, or an archduke at the very least.

Myrrhlock stared into the fire as if he were a creature from the darkest recesses, cold-blooded by nature, that must drink its daily dose of fire and warmth to survive. His face and name were known to Chameol; it had been necessary to take a new shape entirely, and the effort of maintaining the illusion exhausted him. So it was he faced the fire not in the new disguise, or in the twisted shape centuries of spell casting had made of his soul, but in the human form that had once been his true nature, in the far-off century that had been his prime. The face was pale, curiously age-less, hairless, remarkable for its cleft lip. Myrrhlock had removed the goblinstone cap, and underneath it the veins of his skull were raised as if irritated by his broodings.

He stared into the fire as though he sought to find his next action revealed there. His position was, for a time, secure; only the slightest spell of suggestion had been re-quired to establish in the minds of Folderol and his band that Myrrhlock, in his new form, had long been a member of the troupe.

A young girl and a stable boy had nearly undone him; Myrrhlock would not make the error of underestimation again. The conjurer from the marsh was in all likelihood harmless, but there was no sense in chancing again that sort of miscalculation. If he could gain an ally while elimi-nating an enemy, so much the better. Grisaudra would be the monkey, then, that he would send down into the mine after the dark gem he sought.

Out of long practice, the Necromancer no longer needed to say the shape-changing spell aloud; he had only to brood on the runes for it to effect the transformation. Myrrhlock pulled his cloak over his head to shield himself from the light until the metamorphosis was complete. It took some-thing less than a minute before he pushed the hood back and bent to wake Iimogen where she lay asleep at his feet.

It was no more than another minute before she was on her way, clutching the twin to Grisaudra's vial.

Myrrhlock sighed, trying to get comfortable in the shape of his latest disguise. It was not so tall as the shape he was used to, and it was old; the joints ached. He stretched his new hands toward the fire, thought of Grisaudra, and smiled. In order to capture his gem, he must first secure his monkey.

The horses wickered and shifted their weight nervously as Iimogen slipped between them, her young, pale face flashing in the shadows like a small moon. As she drew near to the spot where Grisaudra lay sleeping, Iimogen stepped on a twig and Grisaudra stirred. Iimogen pressed her thumbs lightly to her own eyelids and chanted softly, "Heavy, heavy, three times heavy!" Grisaudra mumbled something half-formed, then sank back into a deep, other-worldly slumber.

Iimogen felt under the pallet, her hand closing around the vial and drawing it out carefully, though there was no danger in waking Grisaudra now. In its place Iimogen left the twin vial, colored and flavored with juniper to match the other but containing another, more singular ingredient. Before she left, Iimogen murmured in the sleeping conjurer's ear. Then she was gone, the only shadow of her passing a ripple of alarm that passed from the nervous horses to the branches of the trees and the fire that flared up suddenly from the slumbering coals.

Grisaudra woke before dawn, her brow damp with sweat. She winced as she sat up and clutched her stomach. It cramped as though she had been given poison. Elric would hear of this in the morning; it was his lousy stew that had done it. Grisaudra had promised herself to be sparing with the cordial; already, when she held it to the light, the vial showed itself only half-full. But these pains were truly awful! She really felt as though she would die unless she had one swallow, comforting and ever so small.

The vision seized her so quickly after she lifted the vial to her lips that it seemed to come out of the bottle itself, like a vapor of evil embodied. It was Myrrhlock, appearing not as the Necromancer with the harelip, nor in his present guise, but in his true form. Centuries of buying off death by eating poison had made of his soul a hideous, scaled thing with unseeing, somehow all-seeing eyes and a mouth of flame.

Grisaudra was held fast by a fascination that was part loathing and part awe. She understood as she stood quaking before him that she was meant to serve him and need not really fear him. That was why she had been made as she had; that was why she had been marked by the sword, so that she might serve one such as this. These thoughts flowed into Grisaudra's mind cold and pure and brilliant as quicksilver, so that she believed they were her own.

The mouth of flame spoke, and the words flared around Grisaudra, bathing her in blue fire.

"Grisaudra, see yourself as you are, as you will be, if you serve me. Look!"

The flames receded and, as though she stood before a looking glass, Grisaudra saw herself unscarred, both eyes grey and wide with light, her unmarred features young and lovely, framed in hair the pale gold of ashwood.

Part of Grisaudra remembered the old wizard of the marsh and a warning he had given her. The way he had died. "No—"

Even with the powerful drug within the drug, Grisaudra still struggled against Myrrhlock. Beauty was nothing to her; it would take a greater prize than comeliness to sway her.

A greater prize Myrrhlock had. The fire flared up to envelop her again, but this time it swirled and formed a figure in fire, the blue flames cooling to reveal a dream-Badger, his limbs still edged with a fiery aura. In his eyes there was desire, and what's more there was love, not for Caitlin, but for her, Grisaudra.

The flames extinguished themselves with a hiss, and the illusion was gone. Grisaudra was weeping. "No."

"Yes. You were made by me, and I made him for you, as your reward.

"But first, you must serve me."

It was as though all her life a cord bound Grisaudra's heart, bound it so tightly that it pained her, and now that cord had suddenly been cut. With that release, Grisaudra opened her eyes and answered him.

In the Gemfields

*I*iliana lay sprawled on the sofa in her chambers, her bronze hair flaming up the sofa back. The queen's eyes smoldered, and she leveled the full fury of her gaze on the goblin in the chair across the room.

Grimald's chin was doubled onto his chubby goblin neck, and his yellow eyes were full of a catlike satisfaction with his day's mischief. Grimald had put in a good morning's work: Iiliana had left him sleeping in the arbor seat only to find, ten minutes later, that he had caught a robin that had hopped too near and pulled out its tail feathers. In the kitchen, where they were making him a new sugar teat, he had managed to pull a whole basin of cooling jam down upon the floor. How he had gotten his little goblin hands into the sewing basket, Iiliana could not imagine. As she handed over the ruined tatters of her best dressing gown to stuff a pillow, Iiliana thought ruefully that it was a hard way to be reminded that a goblin was not a baby, that it grew twice as fast as a human child and had strength to match its cunning.

Still, there was no way to punish him. He was a baby, even if a goblin baby, and too young, or too otherworldly, to warrant a spanking, as much as his actions begged for one.

They had discovered by accident that the goblin could not abide two things, and these were dogs of any size or breed and water. In order to bathe him they had at last to resort to a kind of scouring powder made of sawdust, talcum, and rose petals. Now, when Iiliana had to turn her attention from the goblin for a moment, she left it in the guard of the old toothless mastiff, Pomamber. When the changeling was in the care of the household, the nurse on duty was issued a large sugar shaker full of water, and as soon as the goblin's eyes began to gleam a little too brightly with the contemplation of mischief, the nurse was to sprinkle him with water vigorously, as if he were a newly planted radish patch. The goblin's face would crumple into an expression of alarm and dismay, and it would chew contritely on its thumb for about half an hour.

It was at best, Iiliana thought from her place on the sofa, a temporary truce. Caitlin alone seemed to have any sway with the creature; as soon as Caitlin woke from her nap, she would consult her. Caitlin had fallen into a deep sleep, and for now Iiliana was loath to wake her.

Iiliana was preoccupied by the changeling, or she might have noticed something odd about Caitlin as she lay curled within the warm arm of sunshine from the window. The small mole that had formerly marked her neck beneath her right ear was now to be found beneath the left, and the bruise on her arm where she had hit it on the edge of the washstand had vanished, though a bruise just like it had appeared suddenly on the other arm. If Caitlin had been awake, Iiliana would have seen that her eyes had changed, or rather exchanged, colors: The blue was now green and vice versa. If Iiliana had held a mirror to Caitlin's lips, it would not have misted but darkened, as if a candle flame had been held to it. And a finger touched to the mirror would have shown it to be not soot but quicksilver.

The book of incantations lay beneath the glass, forgotten. Iiliana had replaced the dome over the book without noticing the opening to which the wind had turned. The gilt of the miniature shone as though fresh from the artist's brush,

though this was a part of the book Iiliana had not yet re-
stored. The illustration had been given an entire page, and
it showed Caitlin in a golden robe, holding the goblin baby
to a mirror. Reflected in the mirror was Ylfcwen, clad in
silver and white, holding Bram up to the other side of the
mirror. In the distance, on Caitlin's side, all the inhabitants
of Chameol could be seen, lying where sleep had overtaken
them, the gardener with her shears, the milkmaid upon the
milking stool, her cheek pressed to the cow's flank. The
border of the illustration was a tangled pattern of acrobats
and monkeys.

Iiliana yawned, suddenly unaccountably tired. Or not so
unaccountably, considering the chase the changeling had
been leading her. She could use a nap, at that.

"Pomamber," she called. But the mastiff, asleep by the
door, could not be roused. Without a reliable guard for the
goblin, Iiliana dared not close her eyes. The sun showed it
was early afternoon; she would wake Caitlin. Caitlin knew
how to keep the little fiend in line.

But the queen's eyelids were already shut fast.

Ylfcwen yawned. "It's just not possible," she said again,
as if explaining something self-evident to a very small child.

"He's *mine*; he's my *son*. Don't tell me what is and isn't
possible!" Caitlin's fist came down on the vanity, making
the silver wing-trimmers and bottles of scent dance.
Ylfcwen's opal eyes widened at this display of high feeling.
She reached out with a pale, translucent arm and righted a
toppled bottle.

"It is not possible for *me* to retrieve the bram. If you feel
so strongly about it"—Ylfcwen's tone suggested that feeling
strongly was as distasteful as smelling strongly— "you can
petition Drusian yourself."

The wrath drained from Caitlin's face, leaving it smooth

with sorrow. "Just tell me what I have to do."

The elf queen regarded Caitlin with the sleepy interest that was the closest emotion she had to pity. "It's quite irregular, you know. I myself have not had an audience with Drusian in seventy years or so."

"He will see me."

Ylfcwen raised the silver arch of one eyebrow and laughed, not the formal chuckle used in court, but the intimate laugh used among friends and equals; this distinction, however, was lost on Caitlin. "Stay a little longer among us. Then we'll see whether your confidence will flourish or wither. Don't mistake me! Your determination becomes you. But a pretty dress can become you and still let you perish of the cold."

"I once made my bed in a soldier's barrow under the moor. I've endured winters beyond your imagining. I've known the cold, milady. It's not the cold I fear."

Ylfcwen's opal eyes held Caitlin's uncanny ones in a long gaze. The elf queen was one of the few creatures, human or not, who could bear to hold that look for long. Then Ylfcwen bent and opened a small cabinet by the side of her bed. She extracted and laid out upon the coverlet a small jeweled book, a velvet pouch embroidered with gold thread and pearls, and a small crystal vial on a silver chain.

"The way to Drusian's chambers will take you through the gemfields. The miners serve me, but the other denizens are sworn to Drusian. The jeweled book is the courtbook, out-lining elvish manners and laws; it may assist you when it comes to the goblins and some others you might find. It was my mother's copy, but it is still up-to-date. The bag contains jewels. Where a knowledge of etiquette and the legal code will not aid you, a bribe often will."

"And the vial?"

Ylfcwen picked up her cosmetic scissors and used them to cut a brilliant yellow orchid from the vine twined in her bedstead. She slipped the orchid into the crystal vial and filled the vial with water from a dropper. "This," she said, slipping the silver chain around Caitlin's neck, "is a canary orchid. It breathes even as you do and will sense any deadly ethers in the mines before you can."

Then Ylfcwen went to one of the flower-covered walls of her chamber and opened a hidden door that swung inward with a scraping sound of stone on stone. Elvish engineers would have made a noiseless door, but this was not a door fashioned by elven hands but by others far more ancient, so that the door's scraping was borne by the elves with a little awe.

"Your way is forward," the elf queen said. "Farther I cannot lead you."

Caitlin stepped up to the threshold; it was utterly dark. "Will you light my way, or is that beyond your means as well?"

Ylfcwen chuckled, her laugh the sound of a wayward silver shuttlecock falling into a secret, forgotten well. "If you can't outwit the dark, airling, you've no hope at all of matching wits with Drusian. No, really, it is just that I have no matches on me. All I can send you off with is this." And she placed on Caitlin's cheek a kiss so cold it burned, and when the frosty mark faded, it would leave Caitlin with a smooth, silvery scar, as if she had glued a small mirror to her cheek after some fad of the court.

It occurred to Caitlin, as the heavy stone door scraped shut again, the possibility of treachery, that a creature without scruples would also lack conscience, and that this chamber could well lead nowhere except to her own death.

"But I thought this was only a dream," Newt said disconcertingly in her ear.

"If you're going to talk," said Caitlin, "say something useful. How to light the passage, for instance."

It turned out there was no need; another useful trait of

the canary orchid was that it gave off as a product of its respiration a yellow glow as bright as a lamp.

"Ylfcwen was right," Caitlin said. "The only way *is* forward."

The mine tunnel was nothing like the main corridor. There were no tapestries here. The walls were adorned with the haphazard mosaic of uncut gems, nodes of rubies, sapphires, and emeralds imprisoned in the rock. The floor of the passage was smooth, worn to a high polish by the feet of goblin miners.

Ylfcwen's court etiquette was bound as a girdle book, the binding along the spine brought to a tail that could be tied to the belt, handy for surreptitious consultations during banquets and other problematic social occasions. If he hung by his tail from Caitlin's belt, Newt could read aloud to Caitlin as she walked along the passage.

"Ah," he said, finding the entry he wanted. "Here's a good place to begin."

Goblins

> The old notions about goblins, that they spring spontaneously from coal dust and wet kindling, or that they can spoil milk by looking at it, are now universally discredited, and no one who doesn't wish to look a fool can afford any longer to subscribe to them. In fact, the only things that can be said to be true about all goblins are these: They are the offspring of elves and humans, a human mother being the more usual case, but instances of an elvish mother and a human father are not unknown. Like mules, goblins are sterile, but any other comparisons to the intelligence and brute strength of pack animals are without foundation. The most common goblin features—a ruddy complexion and yellow feline eyes—are various enough to include bluer complexions and green or lavender eyes. Goblins, when not deprived through prejudice of a secure childhood and sound education, display sharp wits and keen minds, often excelling at wrestling, chess, and the writing of satirical plays.

Caitlin gave a small shudder, remembering one of her last conversations with the Badger: *A mooncalf, that's what I am. Now do you see? The blood is bad; bad blood will tell. Monsters breed only monsters.*

"Come now," said Newt, breaking into her thoughts. "He looks nothing like a goblin. You're the one with the uncanny looks. You're the one with a bluish cast to your skin. A cousin on your mother's side, perhaps?"

"Hush," said Caitlin. "I want to hear something else. Read what it says about reading other people's thoughts without permission."

The wild horses of Chameol had wandered brazenly into Iiliana's own vegetable garden and had eaten the last of the lettuces. No one had come to chase them away because all of Chameol was asleep.

The dog lay curled a few feet from the cat it had been chasing when it had been overtaken by the unconquerable urge to sleep. The crows that had been dining on the pie left to cool on the windowsill had fallen asleep on the spot; inside, the pastry cook had pillowed her head on her floury arms while the tarts in the oven hardened into blackened and inedible tiles. In the laundry, the pressers slept on drifts of linen, in clouds of lavender, dreaming of shirts that ironed themselves. Iiliana dozed on the couch in her chambers, dreaming of besting her brother in a snowball fight.

Only the changeling was awake. Grimald sat wedged upright in the chair by pillows, eyeing the mastiff at the door with dismay. Although no one had come to reswaddle him, the goblin did not need changing, for like an owl, a goblin is loath to soil its own nest and will hold its water for days on end, expelling only a few dry pellets. Old wives' tales to the contrary, goblins do not have two stomachs, but they can go for a short time without food, subsisting on the stores of fat that suit them for the cold work of the mines. But despite this natural advantage, Grimald was growing hungry. His ears quivering with the effort, the goblin baby listened with all his might, sifting the several thousand distinct sounds of late afternoon on the island as if turning over the catch from a teeming net. But hard as he listened, Grimald could not make out the singular footfall, the one voice he hungered for above all others. Try as he might, Grimald could not hear Caitlin.

With that knowledge a curious thing happened. Some of the ruddiness left the goblin face, and two fat, golden, resinous tears worked their way out of the corners of those feline eyes. The goblin's silent keening grew greater until at last he opened his mouth and let out a mute and miserable howl. From the depths of her dreaming, the great mastiff covered her ears with her paws and whined. Pomamber alone of all the inhabitants on Chameol could hear the changeling cry.

After he finished the entry on goblins, Newt turned to the first section of the jeweled book, which dealt with niceties of elvish dress.

Attire

Audiences at court call for dress appropriate to the occasion, the rank and station of the person who is to be presented, and the season. One does not go without a wingcase after the first orchid harvest; likewise, it is in poor taste indeed to be seen in any more wing-dressing than a light dusting of crushed pearl *before* it. Binding the wings tightly to the back with linen or lamé is a fashion now deemed not only unattractive but decidedly unhealthy as well. Clipped wings are a certain sign of at least a juvenile delinquent, if not a hardened criminal.

"Heavens!" said Caitlin. "And me in my nightclothes."

"And your toenails want trimming," added Newt. In annoyance, Caitlin transferred the salamander to her shoulder and firmly shut the book.

The canary orchid around her neck illuminated the passage in front of Caitlin for ten strides before the light lost its battle with the pitchy blackness. Far off could be heard the ringing of goblin pickaxes on stone and the high, metallic zithering of mine cars on steel runners.

But where are the miners? Caitlin wondered. The tunnel led on straight ahead, while the echoes seem to come from every side.

"They're mining gems, not coal. If gems were so common, I dare say they would put up signs: EMERALDS AHEAD, SAPPHIRES FOR THE TAKING. As it is, I suppose they're none too eager for you to know where they are."

Caitlin was about to pinch the salamander's tail when she stopped in her tracks, cringing out of instinct, her arms raised against the deadly pounce of some invisible beast. The light of the canary orchid had suddenly picked out of the darkness a thousand fierce and glowing eyes, as if five hundred lions, leopards, and panthers had been imprisoned underground to guard the elven gems.

"It's all right," said Newt in her ear. "They're only stones."

The salamander was right. In this chamber the miners had exposed the deposits of tiger's eye and polished them until they were as luminous and brilliant as amber glass, leaving them embedded in the rough stone of the cavern walls to startle—and warn?—unwary and unwelcome trespassers. Holding high the orchid in its vial, Caitlin could read some runes above her on the wall. They were odd, familiar yet unknown, something like common cat language and yet unlike it. The best Caitlin could make of them was *Hear, O Wanderer, of the great grief of Pj'aurinoor, and the manner of the death of Pj'inkinoor, her beloved.*

"Those are surely not elvish names, nor goblin, either," she murmured.

"No," Newt agreed. "I would say we have come to the first of the guardians we were told about."

"Or warned about . . .?"

Newt bit the lobe of Caitlin's ear, not, it seemed, either to chastise or to comfort her, but to vent his own nervousness.

"But whatever lies ahead of us, Bram is there also, and so there I have to be." With this Caitlin stepped forward into the chamber, and the thousand tiger's eyes followed her movements. There was a carved ivory portal set into the rock, and Caitlin was about to step across the threshold when New't voice, urgent in her ear, made her stop.

"Look again! This is no *mortal* gateway."

Where there had been a moment before a simple ivory arch there now stretched open a pair of gigantic jaws, twelve feet from the sharp point of an upper tooth to its mate below. The ivory seemed quite solid, then just as suddenly it seemed to be made of mist, and the arch was a simple arch again.

The chamber shook with a rumbling, the thunder, perhaps, of a distant rockfall. Perhaps.

Caitlin sat on the cavern floor in front of the arch and began to weep, softly at first and then louder.

The rumbling ceased.

"Why weep ye?" asked a voice played on all the lowest notes of a bass fiddle.

Caitlin raised her head, her face wet with tears. "I weep for Pj'inkinoor, beloved of Pj'aurinoor. I fear he alone could have helped me with my quest."

The ivory arch melted away in mist to show there was no door at all but a pit from which there rose a pungent gas. The light of the canary orchid dimmed and nearly went out.

"There is a passageway to the right," said Newt.

Caitlin found it, hidden in shadow. She had to stoop to enter it, but after a few feet the passage opened into an immense tabernacle of stone, its vast vaulted roof out of sight. The chamber was lit as brilliantly as a summer noon, and the light seemed to come from the sole occupant and the source of the voice, a tigress whose length from ear to tip of tail was that of a village street. Sitting up, the tigress might have eaten sherbet from the crow's nest of a great sailing ship.

All the amber fire of the thousand gems was caught in each of the creature's eyes, and both of these were fixed on Caitlin, so that she almost believed her gown would catch fire from the heat of the stare. The rumble rose again, breaking on its highest note into the deep, musical voice.

"Beg ye no boons of Pj'inkinoor, mortal, for murderers have wiped their boots on his fine stripes and made of his ears tents for their armies. Beg of me, of Pj'aurinoor'j'aurinji, his beloved and mate."

Tiger's Eye

*F*olderol let his hands run through the pile of coins on the tablecloth, scooping up double handfuls and letting them spill again onto the cloth, his mouth in the center of his calico beard pursed into a rosy *O*. Suddenly his eye fell upon Nix, and the old rogue's face underwent elastic contortions from startled alarm to bald-faced greed to murderous cunning, ending in an oily, unnatural smile that was an attempt at beneficence.

Nix's feet were twined around the rungs of the stool as if he were a vine that had grown there, his milkweed hair raked up into tufts where he had twisted it, waiting for Folderol to count out the money and hand him his and Ulfra's share.

"Well, we didn't do as well as yesterday, m'lad, but none too shabbily, all the same. No, not shabby at all. No doubt it's the bad meat that's put the wolves off their form; once they're back on their feet, we'll really be raking it in."

In fact, the take had been considerably larger than the day before, and Folderol would have been cheating them had Nix not already hidden a bootful of coins, mostly silver, in an iron kettle sunk into the earth in one corner of Ulfra's tent.

Muttering and chuckling to himself, Folderol swept a share of the coins off the table into a small sack. Turning to the table behind, he cut a good portion from last night's joint of mutton and handed both sack and meat to Nix.

"Get along with you—that is, before the meat gets cold."
As soon as Nix had slipped through the tent flap, Folderol
leaped up, knocking over his chair and careening around
the room in a crazy waltz. He kicked off a boot and swung
it in a circle over his head, the other hand clapped to his
mouth, his eyes bugging with a suppressed shout of glee.

In the tent, in the bunk below Elric's, the Badger wrestled
with a dream, his face pearled with a cold sweat and his
hair dark with it. In the dream, he was imprisoned in a tower
by a beautiful enchantress. Though her silken hood hid her
face, her voice told him of her cold, irresistible beauty. Every
day she came to his cell with a jeweled casket and taunted
him to tell her its contents.

"Then you will be free," she said.

But he could not even tell her his name. At last, with a
cold laugh, she opened the casket and revealed a braided
coil of hair, black as ink, tied into a noose.

The Badger woke and flung off the blankets, and without
really waking from the dream he found himself across the
room at the table, knife in hand, trying to cut the bracelet
free. In a second, Elric was beside him, knocking the blade
from his hand, a stricken look on his face, as if the Badger
had been about to put the knife to his own flesh.

"Please." The Badger's eyes were bright, as with a fever,
or with fear. "I must cut it off! You must let me!"

"No. I would as soon let you cut your throat."

"I see her in my dreams . . . she's evil, pure evil . . . and
when she opens the box, it's not a bracelet anymore; it's a
noose. . . ."

Elric shook his head, picked up the knife, and set it out
of reach. "I can't say where the dreams come from, but they
are false. Cut the bracelet off and you cut loose your anchor
to reason and happiness, perhaps even to life itself."

The Badger had no more fight left in him. He meekly let Elric lead him back to bed, and he drank the dose of brandy poured out for him without complaint, slipping almost immediately into a profound slumber.

Elric stood over him, watching his features take on in sleep the smooth innocence and simple beauty of a child's, the haunted look gone, as if he were a stableboy again, asleep in the hay of the stable loft.

"He *can't* forget her!" he said aloud. Then he felt a gaze upon him and turned to see Grisaudra watching him from the entrance to the tent, a strange expression on her face.

"He had a nightmare," Elric said. "Go back to sleep."

She seemed to be about to object but turned quietly and went back to her own tent. Elric thought it unlike her to pass up an argument. He hid the brandy and went back to bed himself.

In the morning, the Badger woke and went to feed the horses. He slipped loose bridles on the animals and led them to the watering troughs, where he found Ulfra giving Nix a bath. Sniffing loudly at him that morning, Ulfra had suddenly seized the boy and hauled him off for a rough scrubbing, cuffing him lightly with the palm of her hand if he squirmed too much, working up a lather with cold water and saddle soap.

Ulfra looked up as the Badger approached, her dark hair hanging over one eye, the piercing blue of the other striking a chord somewhere deep within the Badger. Then she shook the hair from her eyes and smiled, a white-toothed grimace and a shrugging of the scalp that was still more wolf than woman.

While her attention was thus distracted, Nix ducked from her grasp and fled, streaming water. The Badger hardly noticed, as his gaze was fixed on Ulfra. She had discarded her soldier's uniform for this chore; as her soaked shift clung to her, the Badger suddenly saw a ghost, tall and dark, wading into the dark surf of the moonlit sea.

The wolf-girl casually spat some saddle soap from her mouth, regarding the Badger curiously from the corner of her eye. He busied himself with the horses, but once Ulfra had gone he clung to the back of the mare, Maud, seeing the figure turn in the surf to cast a glance toward the shore. Her hair was dark but shorn, and while one eye was blue its mate was green. A name played on the tip of his tongue, and then it was gone.

"Are you all right?"

It was Grisaudra, carrying on her arm a basket of goldenrod gathered by the roadside. She had put on a blue cap, and the chill on the morning air had put a hint of roses in her cheeks, so that from a certain angle she might have been a pretty girl of twelve. But the Badger seemed hardly to see her, and when his eyes focused on her face he scowled in annoyance; at the first sound of her voice the vision of the figure in the surf had vanished.

"I'm fine—why shouldn't I be?" he snapped. "Now I've got work to do—as you do."

Grisaudra held her composure until she had rounded the corner of the shed where the horses were stabled. But as soon as she was out of sight, she broke into a run, blinded by tears, and stood sobbing out behind the cooking tent. In a moment she recovered herself and was about to splash her face with rainwater from the barrel when she caught sight of her reflection.

She was the Grisaudra of Myrrhlock's vision; her hood fallen back, hair framing her features in a mist of pale gold. She stood gazing at the reflection until her tears had dried and her breaths came evenly once more. Then Grisaudra gathered up the scattered goldenrod and went to change into her costume for the first performance of the afternoon.

Elric, in the kitchen to beg some matches, stood in the

shadows just inside the tent, his pipe gone cold in his hand, watching her go.

Pj'aurinoor regarded Caitlin out of liquid amber eyes.

"What is it that brought ye to the gemfields of Pj'aurinoor, daughter of light?"

Caitlin knelt in the courtyard formed by the great paws and roofed by the vast chin, a hanging garden of ebony and amber fur. "I am looking for my firstborn and only child."

Pj'aurinoor lashed her tail against the cavern wall, roaring a great oath. A small rock slide rained harmlessly onto the tiger's massive head. Newt, disliking the roaring or mindful of falling rocks, had crept into Caitlin's pocket and was curled there tighter than a stone.

"Hunters!" Pj'aurinoor roared once more. "They took all my children, one by one. My firstborn canopies a queen's bed; now that lady sleeps her widow's sleep beneath that peerless pelt. The others hang in the halls of palaces and fortresses from here to Twelfthmoon. And the youngest, my sweet j'aurinji, dreams at the bottom of the sea, with the cameleopard and griffin, bound for an idle king's menagerie. Hunters!" The whiplash of Pj'aurinoor's tail upset a pile of crowns and boots in one corner of the chamber. "How did thy child come to be taken?"

"Ylfcwen's servant took him in the night and left a change-ling in his place."

The tiger's roar subsided into a low rumble, and she nodded thoughtfully. "A new mother, ye were late giving him a name and then listened to the murmurings of an elvish nursemaid. I have heard the tale before. Where was thy mother, that she did not warn thee of this?"

"The only mother I knew was an old spell-seller in the Weirdwood. The way of the birds she did teach me, but not the ways of men, let alone those of Ylfcwen's race."

"But thyself should have known this, otherworld daughter! Or would ye not heed what was before thy seer's eyes? Where is thy child now?"

"Ylfcwen says he has been taken to Drusian, but who and where he is no one will tell me."

The great tail ceased its lashing and the tiger's throat seemed to have run dry of roars. After a pause Pj'aurinoor spoke.

"Drusian is the Master of Sleep and Desire, whose palace lies two fields beyond this one, past the sapphires and the serpentine. But I fear, daughter of light, that if it *is* Drusian that has claimed thy child, thy best path lies upward, past hope and grieving. Ye are yet young; there will be other cubs."

Caitlin's jaw trembled a little before she lifted it defiantly toward Pj'aurinoor.

"Is that what you did when your youngest was taken? Give up hope?"

"I went and slew the hunters and left only their boots and crowns. But they were hunters; they were mortal. They were not Drusian."

"Is he past beseeching, then?"

"Child, ye would as likely snare the moon in a net of cobweb as to bring back from that chamber what Drusian has claimed." The great chin lowered, and a purring passed through Caitlin like a tremor, leaving her calm and content, so that she could have curled up in the amber fur and slept her life away.

"But I must try," she said, her words muffled by the tiger's fur.

"Yes. The children of light must always do thus: rename the world and reinvent water."

"What would I be, then, if I didn't try?" Caitlin's finger traced an ebony stripe on the tiger's jaw. "His hair is just this color, but softer . . ."

The tiger sighed, a low moan, making her whiskers tremble. "Enough. Child, Drusian rules sleep and desire and rules over such creatures of the shadows as me. I guard this first portal and am sworn to let no human feet trespass here. But if ye were to give me something in payment, it would be no trespass but a toll, and no fault would Drusian be able to find with me. Have ye anything to give?"

"No crowns or boots, I fear. Gems and a book."

Pj'aurinoor snorted her distaste. "Stones and dry leaves— what are these to such as me? Have ye nothing else?"

Caitlin felt in her pocket, and when her fingers closed around the salamander she got a nip, as if to say, Think again! "Just a piece of glass from the sea."

"The flower around thy neck I would take, otherworld daughter. Is it a singing orchid?"

"A canary orchid, but it has not sung for me—more's the pity. But I can't give it up—it's my only light and breath in the gemfields."

Pj'aurinoor lowered her velvet nose, which Caitlin could not have spanned with her hands, to take in the scent of the orchid. Caitlin was lost in a forest of black and amber shadows that smelled of oranges that have lain too long in the sun, sweet and rummy with an edge of tartness. She remembered a morning on Chameol, kissing the Badger, the perfumed oil from an orange rind still on his mouth and hands.

"It has no scent," said the tiger.

"No. Nor a song, either. And I am in no better voice than the flower, I fear. But I can speak you a tale, if I can't sing it in verses. What do you like in a tale? A hunter meeting a grisly end?"

"No—I favor any kind of tale, as long as it has rabbits in it. Ye have told me how the babe was taken, but not how he was gotten. Tell me of thy j'aurinji, thy beloved."

So Caitlin lay in the space between two of the great tiger's toes and told a tale of love found and love lost, how we discover what we love only in the moment that it is taken from us, and learn that the only way to be true to what we love is sometimes to surrender it.

"How lost and how surrendered?"

It was more than Caitlin could bear, to speak of the nights she had nursed the Badger back from the threshold of death, wresting him from the grip of a gilt-and-quicksilver poison. She had made profane promises to the night, to the wolves and the trees and the moon, so that when he woke from the fever she had gambled away everything but two fingers on her right hand.

But she told Pj'aurinoor all of it, how, as they had ridden on toward Ninthstile, she had spent each hour expecting the wolves to come claim their share of her and the branches to pluck out her eyes. The trees whispered but did not reach for her; the wolves howled but did not come within the circle of the fire; and the moon only showed her, in the inky surface of a patch of water, a sight Caitlin had never before seen: the face of a woman in love.

"And how did ye lose him again, child?"

"I found I could not have him and also have knowledge of what I was, what my eyes had made me. I could retain my memory of him but never be with him. Or I might live in the world as if I had never known him. In the end, there was no choice." Caitlin paused, her own face striped by Pj'aurinoor's whiskers, cast into shadows by the canary orchid. Her mouth curled into a small smile. "What a memory it turned out to be! Seven pounds of memory, squalling fit to raise the dead and a shock of hair so black it belonged on a crow—"

The musical thunder of Pj'aurinoor's roar stopped her. "Tell me no more of this tale, daughter of light. Tell me some other, with a sweeter moral to it." The great golden eyes widened into lamps of fire. "Tell me a tale with *rabbits* in it."

"You're sure this will come off?"

Elric twisted around on the stool where he sat, stripped to the waist, an elaborate pattern sketched on his back in charcoal. Grisaudra sat behind him, a crimson-tipped quill poised in one hand.

"Perfectly." She began to fill in the part of the pattern that covered Elric's left shoulder blade, a tangled pattern of roses.

"It's as much as your life is worth if it isn't. Ow!"

"Sorry, but you mustn't move, or I can't answer either for the injury to your back or to the finished effort." Grisaudra consulted the pattern on the table. It was the Badger's handiwork. Within the border of roses he had drawn a figure in a yellow dress, her hair a tangled crown of living eels. In one hand she held a bloodied sword, in the other a red rose.

It was Folderol's idea that the troupe's latest addition should not be merely a bearded duchess, but a duchess with a tattoo. It was he who had seen some of the drawings the Badger made on the backs of old broadsides advertising the leopard-woman who had left to take up dressmaking: horses so lifelike they seemed to rear from the page. Folderol had soon commissioned his trick rider to design a tattoo "fit to make brave men swoon and bring speech to the tongues of the mute." The finished design fit the bill admirably, with a few alterations. The Badger's original drawing had shown the figure's foot resting on a severed head, but Folderol had prevailed upon him to change it to a dragon, which he felt had a more spectacular effect.

Folderol had not seen the other drawings the Badger had made and hid beneath his cot, drawings of the same face over and over from different aspects, but always obscured—by shadow, an upflung arm, a mass of unruly hair—from the viewer's full gaze. It was only Elric who noticed that the severed head in the original pattern for the tattoo bore a disturbing resemblance to the Badger. *Perhaps,* thought

Elric as his back began slowly to bloom with roses, *if he draws long enough, he'll sort it all out and remember that she was anything but a fiend.* For Elric was somehow sure this was not the strange malady at work, but the Badger's befuddled brain trying to make sense of his shattered memories. The drawings were perhaps the best way for him to confront and disarm his demons. They might even be the only way.

Nix had wandered from the place where the troupe was camped and slipped into a farmer's fields. For a while he stood looking at a lamb that had strayed from the rest of the flock, weighing whether it was better to kill it here and have to drag it home or to lead it back and risk someone hearing it bleat. The wolves would much prefer the latter method. At last Nix settled for a couple of geese, twisting their necks when he caught them and stuffing them into a sack. Ulfra liked nothing better than a nice crispy goose, and she let him lick the grease from her fingers.

It was outside the kitchen tent, where he was going to swipe a knife and an onion, that Nix saw something he was not intended to see.

Over a rain barrel was draped a black cloak lined with silk in a pattern of poppies. Nix had no sooner noticed the cloak when a young woman, her clouded-honey hair all disheveled and her eyes wild with terror, came pelting around the corner of the tent. She glanced wildly about her, looking at Nix but right through him, searching the air as if she sought to escape her pursuer through an invisible door.

Just then a man turned the corner after her, the shaven skin of his skull seamed with veins but his features themselves strangely youthful—perhaps it was the quizzical twist given to his mouth by a harelip. He called out a name, and the young woman fell with a gasp to the ground, as if he had thrown a dagger in her back.

The man with the harelip stepped up to her. Snatching the cloak from atop the barrel, he draped the girl in it, muttering a few twisted words in a long-dead rune tongue. The young woman struggled within the folds of the cloak, but she was completely enveloped in it and could not cast it off. She struggled less and less, and her body seemed to shrink with her waning will. The harelipped man picked up what was now a small, fluttering bundle, wrapped the cloak more firmly round it, and turned away, the bundle under one arm.

Nix brought the geese to Ulfra, who cooked and ate them with relish, casting worried glances at Nix as she dispatched the birds. She drew him close to see if a pain or ache had put him out of sorts and caught the unmistakable smell of the Otherworld.

Ulfra curled her lip in distaste and gave Nix over to the eldest she-wolf to be bathed until he should smell neither of the one world nor the Otherworld, but of snow on silver fur, of cooling mutton tallow, of a new-snuffed match. Until, in other words, he should smell completely and entirely of Wolf, and nothing but Wolf.

The Lion Tamer

*H*e blended into the crowd that had come to watch Ulfra put the wolves through their paces, the children making themselves sick on pickled plums and greasy doughnuts, the comely and uncomely there alike to gloat over the freaks, the jaded in search of a fleeting thrill, the timid standing in line for their penny's dose of excitement.

The man in question was grey from his soft felt cap to the dust that covered his boots. His beard and his complexion were grey, as if he were a chimney sweep who could never quite manage to wash all the chimney black away. The only thing about him that was not grey was the color of his eyes. They were black, like soot on a mirror, absorbing everything they saw and casting nothing back. No one seemed to notice him except the vendor who sold him a doughnut, and he remembered him only for the length of the transaction before forgetting him utterly.

He watched with mild curiosity as Nix placed his head in the wolf's mouth and barely raised an eyebrow when the Badger circled the ring backward, leaning from the saddle, a match in his mouth, to strike a light against the sole of the boot of a man in the front row. But when Grisaudra entered the tent and called for a volunteer from the audience, the man was genuinely taken aback.

"Her!" the grey man said under his breath.

Out of instinct, his hand went to the raised welt of an old

scar on his arm. He slipped from the tent and followed the gaudy painted signs to the tent of the tattooed duchess. A sign declared the tattooed duchess to be absent and assured the throngs she would return with five minutes; the man ignored it and slipped inside.

The duchess sat resplendent in a gown of puce silk trimmed with a dark green fringe, enjoying a pipe of clove between showings, her tattoo hidden beneath a shawl. Beneath ginger eyebrows the eyes of fetching grey registered a glimmer of recognition.

"I'm sorry, the tattoo is off view; I'm on my break."

"That's quite all right. It's just that I hate crowds—the smell of hot lard from the doughnut cart was making me sick." While his tone was nonchalant, the black eyes silently asked whether they could freely speak; in answer, the tattooed duchess nodded.

"Something is very wrong on Chameol."

Fear grabbed Elric by the throat, but his eyes were blank when he raised them to the other knight.

"How so?"

"For over a week now, the messenger pigeons we send have not returned. I need hardly tell you, that has never happened."

It had once. One pigeon he had dispatched to Chameol had been delivered to his own door the next morning on a silver plate. The danger was always there. "What else?"

"We sent a swimmer out to try the old ruse of a boy drowning, to draw the dolphins and tie a message to the collar of one of their number. They did not come. But the boy told us he heard them making a strange call."

"In distress?"

"No—almost like snoring, he said it was, if dolphins could do such a thing."

The duchess stroked her jaw in a strangely mannish gesture, absently pulling at her corset where it pinched. "Someone must land on Chameol and see what is befallen them."

"But the Code forbids us to land on Chameol—"

"Yes, normally; but now the need is dire. Clearly, someone must land and send us a message. Have him take precautions against poisonous vapors. He is not to drink or eat anything on the island. A pair of earplugs might be prudent."

The grey man nodded. "There's something else, though. Your fortune-teller, the one with the scar."

"She's a conjurer from the Oncemoon Marsh. Why, do you know her?"

"Yes, but not from the marsh. I knew her fifteen years ago, in the border wars. She was just a kid then, disguised as a boy. It was just before she took the sword in her face that we found out. Little idiot, she stepped in front of the soldier the blow was meant for, a silly sack of vanities, a would-be hero with a pretty face. He was far from grateful; the type seldom is. Her scar was as good as the mark of the devil, as far as he was concerned.

"Anyway, she was sent away with the shroud maker, and next time a sword came looking for that ass's neck there was no one so disposed to step in front of it. It almost broke my heart, the look on her face as she trudged off with that old ghoul. God, to think of her at the mercy of a man who'd sell the gold fillings out of a dead man's mouth. She was a really beautiful kid before her face got in the way of the business edge of a sword."

That evening the Badger was tending to the horses, polishing their coats to a high gloss, then settling down to do the same for the brass bits on the tack. The old lion tamer, Hodge, sat down nearby to watch.

Cleaning tack was the one activity that felt wholly natural to the Badger. In everything else that he did, there was a weird echo, an odd feeling that he ought to be remembering something. This happened several times a day, as he was watching Nix comb and plait Ulfra's hair by the pump or when he caught sight of a woman in the crowd wearing a particular shade of yellow. Sitting down to a supper of hard boiled eggs and the heel of a loaf, the Badger's heart rose in his throat as if it would leap out his mouth. With the brass polish and the rag, there was none of that.

Old Hodge smoked his pipe and watched. The old lion tamer cut an odd figure, with the wild ginger-and-silver mane that fringed his bald pate. He had wide-spaced, narrow eyes and a nose flattened in a long-ago brawl, which combined with his enormous ragged ears to make him look three-quarters lion himself.

Indeed, Hodge was much more frightening to look at than his lion. The broadsides showed Rollo the Man-Eater with a magnificent mane and razor fangs, his eyes great orbs of flame. The true portrait was something rather different. Rollo the Man-Eater was balding around the ears; his belly drooped low to the ground, and in his agitation around crowds he had chewed the tassel off the end of his tail. A very well kept secret (or so Hodge thought) was that the creature wore false teeth and that the great hunks of raw meat delivered to the lion's cage each day were quietly taken by Hodge to be tenderized with a mallet and put through a food mill. And it was not uncommon to find Nix napping, curled head to knees in the fur of the lion's breast, or braiding dried posies of bluebonnets into the thinning mane.

"Where is it you come from? You ride a horse as if you were born to the saddle, but there's something in your way of speaking and the way you hold yourself. You're no stableboy and not even an acrobat, no matter how well you ride."

The Badger shrugged. "I had a mother who had rather grand ideas for me—she sent me off to the monks for an education, and there I much preferred the horses to the homilies. When I wouldn't take the cowl, they sent me off to make my way in the world." All of this was true, but it left out the essential fact that he was now a knight of the court of Chameol. He trusted Hodge; in a way, he reminded the Badger of Asaph, the monk from the abbey at Thirdmoon who had turned out to be a knight after all. But trusting someone and confiding in them were two different things, and the vows the Badger had taken were quite specific about the difference.

Hodge nodded, exhaling a plume of clove smoke. "Ah. So it was the monks who taught you to play the recorder and to draw so true to likeness." Here he gestured to some drawings tacked to the tent pole, of Nix asleep in the lion's embrace, of Elric in full duchess regalia, and one of Ulfra, her arms thrown around the neck of the old she-wolf.

The Badger laughed. "Hardly! Whatever I learned about music and drawing I learned in *spite* of the monks. Or in spite of most of them. The skills they taught were of a different sort altogether. How to sing on an empty stomach at two o'clock in the morning without yawning or letting your stomach growl. Wake me in the middle of the night sometime, and you'll see. Before my feet have hit the floor I'll be on the second verse of a hymn."

Hodge raised an eyebrow in surprise. "To have known you this last week I would never have guessed you had such a laugh in you. What—or who—has made you so sober and so before your time?"

The Badger's smile vanished, and he bent to his work again. "You find me sober?"

"Uncommonly so, for a man young in years, fair-featured, his body untroubled by injury or disease. I can say none of those things with any truth about myself."

"If I am sober, what makes you think there's anything or anyone behind it?"

"Hard to say, though I suppose it has something to do

with the way you are forever twisting that bracelet around on your wrist." Hodge gestured with the stem of his pipe, and the Badger abruptly stopped his absent worrying of the bracelet.

"Yes," Hodge went on mildly, as though discussing nothing more important than the shapes to be found in a passing cloud. "It would explain much, that bracelet. Why you haven't a smile or a glance for the legions of maidens swooning for you. Why you can't tear your eyes away from the wolf-girl."

An image rose in the Badger's brain of an old hag selling eels from a basket. She held in her hand not a writhing eel but a silky skein of ebony hair. Then the memory was gone like a candle snuffed out in a sigh of breath. The Badger came to himself again to realize the sigh had been his own and to find the lion tamer looking at him with mingled remorse and alarm.

"Forgive me." Hodge knocked the contents of his pipe into the fire and flexed his knee, stiff from sitting. "I had no right to dig up those things you have taken such pains to bury. Now I had best go and see what young Nix has been doing with Rollo—probably dressing him up as the tattooed duchess, if I know Nix."

As soon as the lion tamer was gone, the Badger dropped bridle and rag to the floor, pressing the wrist with the bracelet hard between his eyes, willing the vision to return. "Your name! Damn you! Why, *why* can't I remember your name?"

Nix had stolen six toffee apples from the batch meant to be hawked to that night's audience and had lounged in a gluttony-induced stupor while Rollo licked the toffy from his apple, trying not to glue his false teeth together. The wildly content lion licked Nix's face as often as he licked the apple, finding as much toffy in the one place as in the other.

One of the troupe's cats wandered into the lion's cage to pick over the remains of Rollo's dinner. She was a pretty cat with curious markings, orange with black stocking feet and a harlequin mask over her eyes.

"Pretty imp!" said Nix, reaching for her. She fled at his touch, slipping through the bars of the cage and back behind the kitchen tent, where a crow was hopping about, pecking at crusts and cawing a litany of discontent. The racket brought out the cook, a plucked chicken under her arm and a knife in her hand. The old woman cast a sour glance over the boy. She cursed the cat and the crow, kicking the former and throwing a flowered cloth over the other, tucking it under her arm and disappearing into the kitchen tent with it. Nix made a face, his eyes wide.

"Crow pie!" he said to Rollo, who was much more interested in Nix's toffy apple.

That was not, however, to be the crow's fate. For the moment, the cook tethered it to a perch with a piece of twine, muttering a binding spell just in case the bird took it into its head to nip through the butcher's string. The crow hung its head and took up a low cawing that sounded strangely like a woman sobbing. Even more surprising than the tears welling in the bird's eyes was the fact that those eyes were blue. The cook gave the crow a piece of dry cake spread with conserve of violets, or of something that color, and soon the bird had put head under wing.

It was an hour before the evening's performance, but the contrivances on which a convincing performance depended—sulphur pots, a sheep's bladder, concealed wires—lay in a jumble where Grisaudra had flung them the night before.

She ought to have been putting on her fortune-teller's

garb, but Grisaudra sat instead dressed only in her shift, practicing her shuffle with a deck of marked tarot cards. Every time she tried to arch the cards within her hands to bring the interleaved halves together, the deck perversely would spring from Grisaudra's grasp and spell out a fortune of nonsense all over the earthen floor of the tent.

The dice she managed better. The hermit in the marsh had made them for her, carved of mulberry wood for wisdom. He had taught her to use them, too, rolling them to foretell gassy marsh fires or the clinging Oncemoon mists that brought chills, fever, and madness. One thing the dice would never tell her, though, and that was where her family had gone.

Now, as Grisaudra spoke the Badger's name, they came up mustard, for indifference, and ivy, for fidelity.

"Pish-posh! That's off the mark, certainly. Here," she said to herself, "I'll roll them for Elric, and then I'll *know* if they're warped or wormy."

So she said Elric's name over the dice in her cupped hands, shook and tumbled them over the felt-topped camp table. This time they came up borage, for bluntness and courage, and lavender, for distrust.

"That's more on the mark. So, which is it? Indifferent to whom and faithful to whom?" Grisaudra did not throw the dice a third time, not at all sure she wanted a clearer answer to her question.

It was a velvet cloak, faced with silk in a pattern of poppies. Unable to sleep, Hodge had found the cloak on a midnight excursion to the camp pantry. The cloak was hung on a nail behind a net of onions. The lining threw back the lamp's gleam and caught the lion tamer's eye. Hodge worked the bundle loose and shook out its folds.

"Very pretty! Just the thing for the greatest lion tamer in the thirteen kingdoms. A puzzle what it's doing here—can it be the cook's? Does she mean to make rags of it? It falls to Hodge, then, to rescue it. Such a cloak as this is not meant to languish on a pantry hook among the onions."

Pausing to help himself to bacon and cheese, Hodge put on the cloak and wore it back to his tent. Once there, he took out the shears he used to trim Rollo's mane, cut the hood from the cloak, and, turning it inside out, fashioned himself a turban, fastening it with an old shoe buckle.

"Yes—much better to have it pattern side out, as pretty a silk as this. It's a bit dizzying, though. Puts me in mind of the wallpaper favored by a certain hothouse variety of lady. Now, what to do with the rest of it?" He held the cloak up, turning it this way and that, tugging it on the bias to test the stretch, draping it around his middle.

"No—too thick altogether to make a decent sash. Perhaps pantaloons? I'll need to get some butcher paper from the kitchen and cheesecloth to make a test pair with."

The cook looked him over sullenly but handed over the paper, letting him cut all he wanted from the bolt of cheesecloth himself. All the same, Hodge couldn't help wishing as he returned to his own tent that Folderol would find someone else to be the cook. The bread was always hard as bricks, the milk sour, the potatoes green and hard. And her soups, no matter that they burned the roof of your mouth, never seemed to fill or even warm you.

Hodge was not handy with patterns, and it was not too late when he threw the scissors down with a curse and a yawn.

"Glory, I'm weary! This will wait until tomorrow." With that he threw himself down on his cot, too tired even to remove the poppy-covered turban from his head.

Toward morning, Ulfra woke and sat up, shrugging off

the blanket of sleeping wolves. Drawing on her ragged soldier's coat but not bothering to button it or to put on shoes, she crept out into the paling night to look for Nix.

He was curled at the sleeping lion's breast, shivering with cold and fright, as if her light tread and the rasp of the cage door had wakened him from a nightmare. His thin arms went automatically about Ulfra's neck, and he buried his white, milkweed-tufted head under her chin. Ulfra bared her teeth at the smell of otherworld, strong all around the lion's cage. On close inspection, however, Nix seemed to have encountered no terror in the night any more dangerous than a toffy apple.

Ulfra carried the boy back to their tent and tucked the sleeping wolves well around him. Even though he was half-asleep, she fed Nix some rum and milk with a spoon before climbing into bed herself.

But Ulfra slept no more that night. She lay wakeful, shivering at the whistle of the wolves' snoring, starting every time Nix twitched in a dream. When at last it came, never had a creature of moonlight and shadow been so glad of morning.

Hodge was not missed until he failed to appear for the afternoon's first performance. Folderol stormed into Hodge's tent, prepared to sack him for drunkenness, only to find the lion tamer dead where he had fallen.

"Mauled," he said, tossing back a second tumbler of brandy. "Damn, we'll have to poison the lion, and I'll have lost them both. What a rotten morning's work this has been!"

"But surely not Rollo," said the Badger. "For the love of reason, he hasn't a sound tooth in his head!"

Folderol had to admit that. What was more, the lion's false teeth were found on Hodge's nightstand, where he had left them after giving them a nightly polish.

"And surely even *you* don't believe Rollo took his teeth out and polished them and left them there," said Elric.

Folderol frowned. "I might not believe it, and you might not believe it, but the whole rest of the troupe is frightened enough to credit anything just now. It's easier for them to believe in a wild beast returning to his man-eating ways than to believe one of us slipped in with a knife to do him in."

But when Folderol went to the lion's cage, he found the door open and no sign of Rollo. The orange cat sat curled inside the lion's dish, licking the last traces of Rollo's supper from her fur. Nix was questioned, but no amount of bullying or promises of toffy apples could get him to admit to letting the lion out of his cage. The boy only squatted in the dust, placing the doll's saucer span of his hand in the dint, as deep and wide as a soup plate, that was Rollo's paw print.

Sapphire

*T*he knight dispatched to Chameol was a recent recruit, an attempt of Iiliana's to rehabilitate some of the Cavekin, the cast-off children dwelling in caves by the sea and living off the jetsam from shipwrecks. When any among their number began to show signs of "getting big," he or she was unceremoniously turned out into the world, supplying the thirteen kingdoms with a steady stream of pickpockets, horse thieves, and fourth-rate tutors and governesses.

Fiddle, as he was called, had grown half a foot during a summer spent in the saddle and in the classroom, losing his weird Cavekin gibberish and mastering the thirteen dialects of the kingdoms. His sunburn had faded to a rich nut brown, and the attentions of a barber and a dentist had worked wonders. Unlike most Cavekin, Fiddle liked the water and could swim like an otter. This had been the chief factor in his being chosen over all the other knights to investigate the strange silence on Chameol. Scavenging among shipwrecks had made Fiddle an expert diver adept at maneuvering between splintered hulls and slippery submerged rocks.

He treaded water now just off the hidden bay. There was no sign of the dolphins, only a lone seal barking at the sun the way an innkeeper's mongrel barks at the moon. The mournful sound, more than the cold water, made Fiddle shiver.

There were stairs cut into the cliff face, slick with the moss it was someone's daily chore to scour away; Fiddle slipped and nearly tobogganed halfway down again on his belly. He was more careful after that but wished he might have scaled the cliff itself, a simple enough feat for him but one forbidden, as it would have made him too conspicuous.

He scaled the garden wall and dropped silently to all fours in the soft grass, grown quite high. There was a thick silence, as though he were underwater. Ass! he said to himself, shrugging off the creepy feeling. It's only because the birds aren't singing.

Why was it, then, that his heart beat faster the closer he drew to the palace itself? It was white, scoured bright as coral by the sunlight, and there was something about the way the shadows played on its galleries and porches that reminded him of the ghostly hull of a wreck under water. Around him in the garden the ferns swayed in the breeze as if the swells of the sea and not the wind stirred them, and out of the corner of one eye Fiddle took a shower of leaves for the sudden kite's swerve and plummet of a school of fish.

The Cavekin knew the sea often kept the best treasures for herself, and so a few of their number who had grown big were allowed to remain so long as they agreed to dive to the wrecks and bring back highly prized commodities: crocks of gooseberry jam, knives still keen and bright, and the checkerboard they used to divine solutions to all matters of dispute.

Fiddle himself had grown past the mark on the cave wall at which even most divers were cast out. He had been suffered to remain because he knew the wrecks so well and came back with his net bags full of riches: silver spoons, a hand mirror, a waterlogged ham. But one day he came back empty-handed and would never dive again, though he never told anyone why. He had swum through one splintered hull only to come upon a bunk room of drowned sailors, snoring water, counting fish and dreaming of their last breath of air.

Now he half expected to turn a corner in the palace and find them again, and when he saw the first roomful of sleepers his heart nearly leaped from his mouth in fright.

"You fool, Fiddle!" he said aloud. "They're only sleeping."

But it was a sleep from which he could awaken none of them. He slammed windows, stamped around the room, hurled a basin to the floor, and still they slept on. And, half because he remembered it from some old story, but mostly because they were all extremely pretty girls his own age, he tiptoed around the room and kissed them all as they slept.

"It takes a prince, I suppose," he said, shrugging. Fiddle left that room, but not before he had kissed the prettiest again, just to make sure.

He tore down the halls, forgetting all knightly caution, hallooing at the top of his lungs, when he turned into a doorway and found himself in the chamber where Caitlin lay asleep. It was a long moment, his heart thrumming, that he stood by the door, summoning the courage to approach the bed where her blue-black hair lay spread on the pillow. When at last he did, Fiddle was too scared to kiss her and could only step up and shake her. But his hand passed all the way through her shoulder, though she looked solid enough, and he felt the mattress beneath. The hair stood up on the back of Fiddle's neck, and he backed out of the room on tiptoe.

The cheek had quite gone out of him by the time he found Iiliana. Her room was full of pigeons, perched on the frame of the mirror and on the canopy of the bed and even on Iiliana's shoulders where she dozed on the sofa. Each bird wore an unanswered message on its leg. Fiddle did not need to read them to know what they said. Some of the pigeons, having eaten everything else in the room, had started to peck at the cakes of rouge and crumbs of talc on Iiliana's dresser.

Grimald was asleep, too, though out of exhaustion rather than enchantment; his squalling had worn out even a goblin's considerable stamina. Fiddle looked at him and, not seeing his goblin's eyes, thought him only a particularly ugly baby.

Fiddle roused Pomamber, murmuring in her ear a promise of giblets and gravy. The mastiff padded down the hall after her newfound benefactor, it taking something much stronger than enchantment to keep a dog and a boy from ransacking a pantry when the whole of a household is asleep.

Caitlin and Newt left Pj'aurinoor half asleep, her eyes narrowed to crescent moons, growling happily into her whiskers about rabbits.

As Caitlin made her way out of the fields of tiger's eye, Newt twined his tail tightly in Caitlin's belt and read aloud another passage from Ylfcwen's court etiquette.

Tipping

It is a grave insult to tip anyone of full elvish blood, and customs vary widely regarding gratuities for goblins. One can never go wrong, however, in leaving a tip for weavers and other human interlopers. The preferred currency is dried jasmine flowers or dragonfly wings; when the interloper has accrued his weight in these, he may purchase his freedom: a plain brown suit of clothes and passage to the surface. In practice, this is seldom done, since most interlopers returning to the human realm are taken for madmen and conducted to the nearest asylum. (An exception to the rule about tipping among elves is granted on the evening before the feast ushering in the orchid harvest, on which occasion elven young give their elders silver pieces of human minting, which are then melted down and fashioned into useful implements.)

The passage made Caitlin shiver, for it put her in mind of a man she had seen once, in the days she lived in a barrow on the moor. She had met him in the marketplace; he was raving outside a baker's shop. His skin had a phosphorescent pallor and his eyes an uneasy brightness, and he wore a suit of clothes the color of earth. He had not fled at the sight of her, a witch in bells, and when out of pity Caitlin had pressed on him some of her own bread he had laughed, filling her hands with glimmering moondust from his pockets: wilted flowers giving off a crushed fragrance, a powder of dragonfly's wings.

A nip on her earlobe brought her back to herself. Newt had regained his perch on her shoulder to murmur, "Where are we?"

Caitlin held up the canary orchid; its glow brightened but showed nothing but the same passageway, paved with uncut gems, such as they had traveled along since leaving Ylfcwen. *How much further it is we have no way of knowing*, she thought. Caitlin had a sudden uneasy vision of herself emerging at last into the final chamber, an old woman, to find Bram already a grown man with no memory of his mother.

Enough of such elvish thoughts. Newt chided her gently, but did not bite Caitlin's ear. *As the elf queen said, our only way lies forward.*

It was a workday like any other. The goblins descended by cart into the depths of the gemfields and upon reaching the appointed site assembled in rows, while their captain led them through the oath of allegiance. Then Ylfcwen's silver banner was raised on a pulley set into the rock, the canary orchids set into recesses in the wall, and pickaxes began to ring on the stone.

They were working emeralds today. The captain sorted the rough stones by size and grade, the poorer ones destined for a workshop that would turn them into chips for mosaics and beads for embroidery. Gems larger than a fist were set aside to be taken to Ylfcwen; all the rest were piled into carts to be sent to the lapidary.

One goblin, taller than the rest, paused to lean on his pickax, listening to the sound of the mine carts on the runners, remembering the tales his father had once told him of sleigh rides through the snows of Ninthmoon that made him deaf with the wind and numb from the cold and blinded by the eddying snow. His father was one of the weavers, his mother none less than Ylfcwen herself; with such a pedigree the goblin might have remained at court and enjoyed all the privileges and favors due one of the queen's favorites. But he preferred the company of goblins to that of elves; the whole court seemed to him to reek of the slow decay of orchids, and the sight of his father, blank eyes in a face flushed with root wine, made his blood rage.

The miner picked up his ax and soon fell into the rhythm of the other pickaxes. He had not struck a dozen blows when the captain blew a short blast on a whistle pitched too high for human ears, and the lamps were doused and the goblins took cover under the rubble and in side tunnels. The elf queen's son did not grumble with the rest, though he didn't like these trespasser drills any more than the others.

On this occasion it proved not to be a drill. A human tread echoed in the tunnel, and the miner barely had time to shrink into the darkness when a woman passed within a few inches of his hiding place. The canary orchid around her neck showed the woman's face, a perfect moonstone set with a sapphire and an emerald. She was soon lost in the shadows along the tunnel, and in a moment two long shrills of the whistle declared the all clear. Soon the miner had entered into speculation with his neighbors as to what the lunch cart would bring that day.

Bram woke in a black, chill silence, drew a breath to cry, and could only sigh and shudder.

A hand, white as death and cold as stone, drew over the child a blanket of ravens' feathers. Bram's eyes closed as though they had been drawn shut, and he slept.

On a nearby table lay an inlaid game board, and on it stood game pieces of ebony and lemonwood. A mirror of crystal, highly polished and hinged like a book, stood open in a bookstand. On the pages images and words formed, swirled, and reformed. When the hand reached out to touch the page, the image was frozen: Caitlin lifting the canary orchid to light the tunnel, Grisaudra tattooing Elric's back, Ulfra and Nix resting among the wolves, Grimald and Iiliana sleeping while a cloud of pigeons rose and settled around them.

The hand rose again to lift a game piece of ebony, moving it from a part of the game board set with tiger's eyes to a part inlaid with sapphire. Bram stirred and sleepily kicked the blanket of feathers from his legs. The hand, veins empty of the blood of humans or of elves, a hand enormously old but without the signs of age, drew the blanket of raven feathers carefully back into place.

Everything before Caitlin suddenly turned blue. The tunnel opened into a wide chamber paved with cobalt and lighted through panels of blue stone set into the ceiling. It was like being beneath the waves; Caitlin felt a sudden memory of weightlessness and the embrace of seaflax and the seal's bristly kiss.

The floor of the chamber, too, might have been at the bottom of the sea rather than deep within the earth: old sea chests gaped to show rusty maws full of pearls, and the strange shapes of the rocks might have been coral. There was a large rock in the corner that looked exactly like an old man bent over a book.

Just then the rock looked up, and Caitlin startled so that Newt lost his grip and barely caught hold of the hem of her robe on the way down.

"You're not blue," he said in a voice of displeasure. The old man was blue, with a face like blue cheese and eyes like cornflowers and fingernails so dark he might have lived on nothing but blueberries. What of his hair was not covered by a pointed cap was the blue of wood smoke. Even his tongue was blue.

"Just the one eye, I'm afraid," she said. "These must be Ylfcwen's sapphire fields."

"Oh, not Ylfcwen's!" The old man blushed indigo. "No one owns these fields but Drusian. Ylfcwen may by rights mine them, but she by no means *owns* them. What is your name, then?"

"Caitlin."

"You may call me Cerulean; it's as good as any of the others. Have you any blue blood in you?"

"I was left in the woods as a baby, so it's as likely to be blue as any other color. It's certainly blue now, from cold if nothing else."

Cerulean stirred up the blue fire and bade her come forward to warm herself at it. As she stretched her hands toward the heat, Caitlin saw Cerulean had been writing in a great book. The old man drew a blotter over the page before she could do more than see it was an inventory written in blue ink in a small, neat hand.

"Just some jottings—only my little game. Are you quite warm now?"

"Yes—am I far from Drusian's chambers?"

Cerulean would not meet Caitlin's eye as he answered. "Oh, one would always hope to be far from those chambers! You are quite near, if you really mean to reach them. What business do you have there?"

"Something of my own to reclaim. Are you a toll-taker for him, too?"

Cerulean sighed. "No—nothing that happy! I stole from Drusian something of incalculable age and immense power—pawned my soul for it. A stone—"

"A sapphire—?"

The old man's eyes snapped, and he shook his head. "More than a sapphire! The Bluenose—the seer's stone smuggled out of Th'teenmoon by the queen who was young Unger's bride. She dressed as a crone and hid the gem in a potato. It was lifetimes later I chanced on it—and stole it. But not from human hands; at least, not living ones. I was a relic-seller then—a grave robber, to call the calling by its true name."

Caitlin remembered another relic-seller she had known, and her hand went out of habit to the spot at her throat where her catstone had once nestled. Instead of touching the amulet, her hand closed on Newt, who had curled his feet in the lacings of her bodice and was pretending to be a pewter brooch of a dragon.

"As a punishment, Drusian set me to a task so immense I shall never finish it: to complete *The Book of Blue.*"

Caitlin knew of it: a long nonsense poem begun by a king mad with grief for his dead bride, a young queen with blue eyes. It was a book long lost, sought out by seers who in reading it hoped to find wisdom among the madness. Between love poems to his wife, the king had begun a catalog of blueness, a list of all the shades, from smoke to steel to thin milk, a census of everything blue.

"It would have been easier to set me counting all the stars in the heavens or all the grains of sand on the shores of the sea. Take *blue-cap*, now. It can signify a serving maid, a titmouse, a cornflower, a kind of ale, or a sort of worthless blue stone."

Caitlin's mind was hatching a plan; whether it was to be successful rested on whether Cerulean still possessed the soul of a relic-seller.

"What would you give," she asked, "for the name of a new blue thing?"

"Much, if there was such a thing. But"—here Cerulean sighed—"I wouldn't wager much on it."

"Would you wager passage to Drusian's chambers?"

Cerulean took off and twisted his pointed cap, as if trying to wring an answer out of it, then punched it into a cone again and pulled it down over his ears. "Not to those chambers. You must pass through the field of serpentine first. But I will tell you the secret for passing safely to Drusian's very portal. In return you must name something blue that is new to me."

"And if I cannot?"

"Then you must take my place and copy out for me a page of *The Book of Blue.*" Cerulean rubbed his hands together. "Agreed?"

Caitlin smiled crookedly. "Beware such barters, old man. I bartered with a relic-seller once and lost. But the relic-seller lost even more. If I relieve you, how do I know you'll come back or that I won't finish the page to find a few hundred years have passed? Remember, my business is with Drusian. Surely," she said, lowering her voice a notch, "you would not risk his wrath?"

Cerulean wadded his cap into a ball. "You would copy only

a page—so that I might creep so far as the edge of the sapphire field and glimpse a bit of something *green. . . .*"

Looking around the chamber, Caitlin felt a pang for him, imagining how relentless the press of blue must be on Cerulean's eye—as well as on his reason.

"Very well," the chronicler of blue said, composing himself a bit. "Let's begin. Tell me of something blue."

Caitlin's eye fell first on the blue columns of *The Book of Blue.* "On Chameol, there is an ancient runebook and in it—"

Cerulean interrupted her with an impatient wave of his hand. "Yes, yes, yes: three ribbons, one-green-one-silver-one-blue, and a forget-me-not pressed by you when you were six years old between the eighty-second and eighty-third pages. And a blue moth that met its end napping on page four hundred one." Cerulean looked at Caitlin balefully. "I thought you were going to tell me something *new.*"

Newt's teeth nipped Caitlin, pinching her through the stuff of her gown. *You ought to know better than to underestimate a relic-seller. That's how you lost your amulet the first time.*

Well, if you're quite through napping, you might lend a hand, she answered crossly. *Some seer's glass you are.*

Newt's only answer was to fill Caitlin's mind with a picture of her old barrow on the moor and of a long-dead warrior's ring set with a blue stone. Again, the words were hardly out of Caitlin's mouth when Cerulean broke into her tale.

"—and inscribed To ALFRED, with a small chip on the stone." Cerulean flipped through a few pages of *The Book of Blue* and ran a finger down a column. "Here it is, under 'Tokens of Affection, Miscellaneous Rings.'"

Caitlin began to despair a little, and in her nervousness her hand crept to the spot where her cat amulet had lain, closing on the glass salamander. Instantly, she was among the seals again, in the gold and dark-green fronds of the sea-flax, hearing the seal speech she had so quickly forgotten, understanding it again. What she heard was a tale like a remembered dream. Submerged in so much blueness, Caitlin's green eye seemed to give out the only light in the room.

"Not a year ago a bundle was thrown from a sailing ship, the *Double Dolphin,* some oddments wrapped up in cloth and tied with a leather lace."

"You are going to tell me, I suppose, what was in the bundle?"

"Two things, I know: the others I can guess. A prayer-book, to give it the weight to take it to the bottom; a recorder, broken in half. Two things I would stake my life were in it: two glass marbles, one green, the other blue. This bundle sank to the bottom of the Strait of Chameol, where it came to rest at last in the belly of a whale, and it rests there still."

This was not entirely true. Unknown to Caitlin, the undigestible bundle had caused the whale a great deal of discomfort, and after a few hours of indigestion the creature had expelled the bundle with such force that it split open. The prayerbook had sunk to the bottom, puzzling the ancient eels before it was furred over with sea grass. One marble, the green one, made a fisherman rich, for many would pay to wonder at a lobster pulled from the sea with a glass eye. Of the blue one, nothing more was known, above or below the waves.

It was enough for Cerulean. Well pleased, he blued his tongue with the nib of his pen (or inked his nib on his tongue), and entered the story of the marble in his venerable catalog, under "Talismans, Lost and Mislaid."

Caitlin had heard the tale from the seals, and her own knowledge of the Badger had filled in the missing details. If he had had hair enough to cut or a sealskin to shed, he would have undertaken such a metamorphosis. As it was, the only way he could think of to purge his heart was to send every remnant of the past, every memory of Thirdmoon and especially of Caitlin, to find its rest among the coral porches and watery gardens of the sealfolk.

Cerulean had to touch her shoulder to bring her to herself and tell her the safe way through the fields of serpentine.

"Do not trust your eyes there, not even if they're seer's eyes. What is down is up, and what is not can seem very real. Do not go forward or backward, left or right, but in the one direction you think you cannot go, for that is the only safe way."

That was all the warning he would give her; when Caitlin left him, she was still uncertain whether Serpentine was a gem or a person or some other kind of creature. She did not guess it named all three.

"So," Newt said, when they had left Cerulean to his task. "What sort of seer's glass do you think I am now?"

"Still an odd one. You've shown me the past as often as you've shown me the future."

"Hmm." Newt twined his toes in Caitlin's hair. "The one world doesn't know what the Otherworld is doing."

"What is that supposed to mean?"

"Just that running pell-mell into the Otherworld may bring you up short, face-to-face with your past. There was a time before these walls were built, when the one world and the Otherworld were the same, when memory of the future was not a gift given to seers alone. Though I wonder, sometimes, whether you have such a gift at all, to rise to Ylfcwen's bait like a whippet after a stuffed hare."

"Bait? What do you mean?"

"Has your love of Bram so blinded you that you can't see you're the prize they want?"

And no matter how Caitlin cajoled and threatened him, Newt would say no more; he curled tight into a ball and went to sleep.

· E L E V E N ·

The Fire-Eater

*I*t was a source of no little amusement to the rest of Folderol's band that Pyle, the fire-eater, did not like any spice in his food. He waved away the pepper mill and would not partake of anything that was hot to the palate; none, in other words, of the Badger's favorite foods. To the Badger, raised on such abbey fare as suet pudding, the spices and relishes of the taverns and courts had been a revelation. Grisaudra had brewed him a bottle of hot sauce to render the cook's green potatoes and watery soups edible.

"Well!" said the Badger, swinging a leg over the bench where thin, sallow Pyle was sitting. "If it isn't the fire-eater who would eat no fire!"

"Wait and see," Pyle replied with placid good humor. "When you go, the apothecary will open you up and find your stomach as full of holes as a sieve."

The Badger grinned and uncorked the bottle. Across the table, Elric eyed the concoction and tried to conceal his unease. He did not like the idea of Grisaudra brewing potions for anybody, even if the only power they had was to raise a blister on the roof of one's mouth. He had been able to think of no way to caution the Badger without alerting Grisaudra, and there had been no opportunity to replace the stuff with a bottle of pepper sauce bought in town. So far, the Badger had suffered no ill effects from this latest potion of Grisaudra's. Apparently all the spell-seller had added to the mixture of vinegar and honey and pepper was her own devotion.

The fourth ingredient seemed to have had as little an effect as the other three. The only object that seemed to excite the Badger's imagination was Ulfra. There was something about her, something in her wolvish gait, in the mane of dark hair, in the narrowed ice-blue wolvish eyes, that was a magnet for his gaze. The Badger scolded himself: *She's just a child, and half-wolf at that.* But the sight of her, wandering the edge of the camp at dawn or dusk, dressed in her soldier's coat, her arm around the neck of the old mother wolf, made the Badger's throat go dry.

One of the acrobats, Magda, had taken Ulfra under her wing and taught her some tumbling tricks. In the process Ulfra had lost some of her bent-kneed gait and had begun to walk with a grace that said "woman" as much as "wolf." Magda had given Ulfra the present of a hairbrush, which Ulfra used on the wolves until shown a better use for it one day after an accident with some honey. Once Nix had coaxed the worst of the snarls out, Ulfra found she enjoyed having her hair brushed. She rejected Magda's well-meant gift of a gown but did surrender her soldier's coat for a riding kit, breeches and a fitted jacket of green leather.

But Folderol did not want his wild wolf-girl to look too tame, lest the troupe's take suffer, so before she entered the ring Ulfra took her hair out of its plait and used a little honey hairdressing to lend the proper feral dishevelment.

Neither Elric nor Grisaudra was much pleased with the blossoming of the wolf-girl. Elric worried that Caitlin's memory could not hope to regain its place in the Badger's heart if Ulfra had replaced her there. To Grisaudra, Ulfra was a dangerous rival for the Badger's affections, nearly as like Caitlin as any apparition Grisaudra could conjure with all her drops and potions.

That evening Elric stopped by Grisaudra's tent while the Badger was giving the horses their evening hot bran and cod-liver oil. He found the conjurer seated at a small folding table, her marked cards spread out before her in the crossed-star pattern of a love-fortune. As Elric came in, she swept the cards into her lap and looked up.

He did not wait for an invitation but drew a chair to the table and took his seat. "I think it's time we gave the Badger another dose of those drops of yours."

Grisaudra looked genuinely startled. "Why?"

"Have you watched him lately?" *But then, when did you ever tear your eyes away?* "He takes his eyes from her long enough to catch a good wink's sleep. I swear, if she were to dive off the edge of a cliff he'd plunge right over it after her."

Grisaudra stared thoughtfully into the fire. "You said the only cure for his amnesia would be for him to remember her on his own."

"Well, if we don't do something soon, he may *never* remember her. He'll fall in love with Ulfra and raise a pack of howling brats with noses too sharp and ears too big to be canny."

Grisaudra abruptly stood and began snatching bundles of dried herbs from the tent pole as if racing to take washing down from the line before a storm. She began to crumble the herbs between her hands into a bowl.

"I've never used the drops twice on anybody before. There's no telling what might happen."

Elric laughed unkindly. "No, no telling *what* might happen! Heaven forbid, he might even *remember* her."

Grisaudra did not look up, but she stopped rolling the dried leaves between her palms to crush them. "And just what do you mean by that, pray tell?"

"Oh, come now, Grisaudra. Tell me, which is it you take me for, a blind man or a fool?"

"Mad, for as much sense as you're making at the moment."

"All right, I'll spell it out for you: You won't give the Badger the drops because he might remember Caitlin, and where would that leave you?"

She laughed. "I was wrong. You're mad *and* a fool."

"I think not. I've been watching you ever since you showed up so conveniently when he was taken with fever. I was afraid that pepper sauce you'd brewed up for him was poison, but now I know it can't be anything stronger than a love posset. God, what an idiot I was to take the poor wretch to you in the first place!" The look on her face was something awful, but Elric's tongue had run away with him, and he could not stop.

Grisaudra flung out an arm blindly in Elric's direction and sent the bowl of herbs skating off the end of the table, scattering pottery and releasing the bruised fragrance of late-summer meadow. The blood seemed to drain from her face, and she gripped the edge of the table so tightly that the veins stood out in her hands like cords.

"Couldn't I say the same of you?" she said in a low voice. "Perhaps Ulfra will bring Caitlin's memory to life again and leave you no chance to woo her yourself. But with the drops, there would be the chance he could be made to believe Ulfra *was* Caitlin. . . ."

"You're crazier than even I gave you credit for being."

She laughed. "It's no use denying it, Elric. I didn't need to steal a hair from your pillow to divine *that*. Did you know that you talk in your sleep? Shall I tell you what you say?"

He lunged for her across the table but succeeded only in toppling the wooden rack of vials that held the various extracts and oils Grisaudra used for composing her drops. Elric turned his head too late and caught the splash of stinging liquid in his eyes.

Grisaudra grabbed the pitcher of rainwater and tried to bathe his eyes, but Elric shook her off.

"You'd better let me. Heaven knows what's got in your eyes out of that mess."

He only stared at her with an awful look. What he saw, Grisaudra could only guess; the accident had married changeable oils and distilled marsh vapors that she herself would never have dared combine. They stood and stared at each other in a terrible silence, and then he turned and was gone.

Grisaudra began to sweep up the scattered herbs to see whether there was anything worth saving. But the smell of their crushed sweetness conjured up her own imaginings, in which the Badger and a summer meadow figured greatly, so that the sight of the chair Elric had overturned made the conjurer burst into bitter tears.

It was a mercy to Elric to find the Badger absent from the tent they shared. God! He was shaking like a man who had seen a murder or done one. In the bit of mirrored glass that hung over the basin he looked murdering mad.

"Damn her!" Whether he was damning Grisaudra for her shrewdness or Caitlin for unwittingly making a misery of his life, Elric himself wasn't sure.

Had he really allowed himself to fall in love with her? And was he really so mean of spirit and small of heart to wish the Badger's memory away, so that with time and persuasion Caitlin might be taught to love another? On Chameol, even to speak such a thing would be enough to lose him his knighthood, earn him banishment. This was the mystery, though: that Elric had long felt himself a man stripped of his best reason for living, had felt dishonored, disowned, and disgraced, a man banished to the edge of madness. Would he really have come so close to striking Grisaudra if she in turn had not struck a nerve?

The Badger came in from tending to the horses and looked at Elric curiously.

"Are you all right?"

"Do I look otherwise?"

"A little ragged around the edges. You winced when I came in."

He pleaded an earache and had to force down the toddy the Badger brought him, had to swallow, too, the gossip the Badger told him to mask his concern. The Badger had sweetened the wine with honey, but Elric thought the bitter taste of his guilt would choke him all the same. He wished he might forget for a little while the woman another man must be brought to remember loving.

The drops, after all, had only shown him Caitlin stumbling through the snow, a pack of farmers' hounds at her heels. As the toddy lulled Elric off to a fitful doze, the scene continued in his dreams, only now it was Ulfra leading her wolves on a chase through the winter woods.

After he had dosed his patient, the Badger went out. He found Pyle at the makeshift forge set up to shoe the horses.

"I was a farrier, you know, before I fell in with Folderol. But I didn't like it much. There wasn't a living to be made in horseshoes, and I hated to feed my family with bread made from swords and armor." Pyle laughed, turning a small piece of iron he was working in the fire. "In the end, though, I was put in debtor's prison, and when I got out my wife and children had moved on. The Widow Pyle, they called her! I suppose when you go to debtor's prison you *are* as good as dead."

Pyle took the tongs from the fire and did some delicate hammering and cajoling of the hot metal, returning it to the fire briefly before plunging it into the trough of water.

"That is a good way to start, if you've any ambition to be a fire-eater. You have to know the uses of fire before you can begin to master its fancies and deceits. There," he said, "I think we can take a look now."

It was not a cloak pin, as the Badger had thought, but a

hair clasp formed of an intricate iron knot.

"Here," said Pyle, handing the Badger the tongs, "take a closer look."

In the lamplight the Badger could see in the pattern of whorls and knots the stylized head of a wolf.

"For Ulfra?"

"Yes. I thought these recent improvements should be encouraged. I have a bit of a soft spot for Ulfra; she reminds me of one of my daughters." Pyle took the ornament and turned it over in his hands, hands too callused and scarred over to be burned. Then the fire-eater threw back his head and laughed, a robust guffaw surprising from one so thin and sallow. "Ah, yes," he said, wiping his eyes. "She does remind me of Penny. Penny never *would* wash."

The Badger stood and shivered at the sight of the smoke and steam rising in the mingled lights of the lamp and the moon. The smell of hot iron had brought streaming back a hundred kindred sensations from his days at the abbey: the smell, like burnt hair, of the hot shoe put to the hoof; the whine of the knives on the knifegrinder's stone; bells calling him to prayers; the cock's crow, to chores; and the whispered absolution of the old mare in his ear.

The memory struck him with the force of an actual blow: the nape of a woman's neck where the plait begins, the back of the neck of a woman seated before him on a horse.

The vision was gone as quickly as it had come; even as he tried to fix the picture in his mind it was lost, the edges lost first in a grey mist and finally in a black shadow.

Pyle's hand on his shoulder brought the Badger back to himself. Pyle looked at him closely.

"Seen a ghost?"

"In a manner of speaking."

He turned away from Pyle's tale of a knifegrinder turned sword swallower as soon as he could without being rude.

Once out of sight, the Badger paused to lean against a sign he had painted for Folderol, showing Ulfra dressed in a wolf's skin. You MARVELED AT THE LEOPARD-WOMAN, the sign bawled in crimson lettering. NOW BE ASTONISHED AT THE WILD WOLF-GIRL AND HER PACK OF DIREWOLVES.

The Badger rubbed the inside of his forearms, suddenly remembering the rasp of rough wool against his skin as he had reached his arms around her to hold the reins. The wind had blown the sting of sea salt into his eyes and whipped strands of ebony hair into his face. The Badger stared at his own handiwork, the picture meant to draw crowds to see Ulfra. It was really nothing like her. Too old, for one thing; for another, Nix had upset the blue paint pot, so the Badger had had to use green for the other eye. No, it was nothing like Ulfra at all.

Nix liked to watch Pyle swallow his "savory," the small bit of fire he ate for luck before going to bed. He would take a little lamp oil and brandy in his mouth, then ignite the mixture from a flaming torch. The amount had to be exact, so that the fire would have burned itself out without burning through to his tongue and throat. Each time he did this, whether for practice or before paying patrons, Pyle would swallow a spoonful or so of lamp oil, and over the years this had taken its toll on his liver. This was the reason he took no artificial fire with his meat. In a short time Pyle knew his liver would force him to give up this line of work and go back to shoeing horses.

Pyle now exhaled a curling stream of fire several feet into the air with no more concern than if it had been a plume of pipe smoke. Blowing fire rings was one feat he vowed to do before he retired, but as yet he had not mastered it.

The fire now out, Nix handed Pyle a tumbler of milk. This

ruined the effect on stage, but in practice Pyle allowed himself the soothing tonic.

"You're surely a strange kid. Why don't you ever say anything, I wonder?" the fire-eater mused aloud. The brandy worked Pyle's brain as much as the lamp oil vexed his liver, but Nix ignored this address and only put out a finger to nudge the torch and tickle the flask of lamp oil and brandy.

"I bet you could tell some tales, if you wanted, you and the wolf-girl. And so could I, if I had a mind. Queer doings I've seen around here, queer indeed. No fewer than two knights of Chameol hiding out in Folderol's band—and I should know; I was one myself, once, and would be still, if I'd a steadier head and a stouter heart. And both these knights traveling, mind you, in the company of a Oncemoon spell-seller with the face of an angel the devil took a dislike to. More of that one is for sale than her spells, unless I'm very mistaken, and I mean her soul, not just her famous curative embraces!"

Nix blinked and only sighed as Pyle confiscated the flask of lamp oil and brandy and offered the boy the rest of the milk instead. Nix drank, his hands small around the tumbler and his eyes huge over the rim of it.

"Knights of Chameol. I could indeed tell them a thing or two." Pyle rubbed his chin and let out his odd, outsized guffaw. "Yes, I've half a mind to— Come, lad, help me put all this away. I've an errand to run to our friend the duchess."

Pyle's summons found the duchess still awake.

"All right, I'm up! No—we'll talk outside. You've awakened the dead, but one of the living's still asleep, at least."

Leaving the Badger to his slumbers, they went outside.

"And what is this errand that's so important that you must rob me of my beauty sleep?"

"A proposition."

"Oh my. Tell on."

"Oh, I shall," Pyle murmured into his collar. "I've a barter for you. Some information in return for a favor."

Elric shrugged; he'd come out without a shirt, and the shrug made the woman tattooed on his back appear to shudder, her tresses of living eels to writhe. "Tell me what sort of favor you think I have in my power to grant. As far as money goes, I'm afraid you'll find me a duchess much gone down in the world."

"No, something minted in a richer metal. A knighthood."

Elric bowed, grinning. "In the Order of Gawk and Grimace?" These were the caricature knights of the puppet shows.

"Indeed not. In the Order of Chameol itself."

Keeping his face carefully the same, Elric laughed. "They're one and the same: a child's fancy and a fool's figment. Come, man; whatever it is you've been drinking, I want a sip!"

Pyle snapped his fingers and a flame sprang up and danced in his palm; he snapped them again and it was gone. Elric felt the hair rise on the back of his neck.

Pyle wagged a scolding finger at him. "Now, now. What would Iiliana say to hear you speak so?"

The lady on Elric's back tossed her eerie curls again. "You've robbed some old magician of his tricks, bribed some drunken fool of a few meaningless passwords, and you've taken some wild notion that it should all mean something to me. Tell me how I should be impressed."

Pyle took out a pipe and lit it with a snap of his fingers. "Is that a brother's love, to call his sister a meaningless password?"

Elric wondered through the layer of cold composure that lay over his panic how on earth Pyle could have learned any of it. The harlequin cat—the one that liked to kill songbirds—hissed and scared Elric out of his wits. He swore and kicked it away, thinking, I never even saw it. Where did it come from?

"Think, brother!" Pyle whispered urgently. "How else could I know these things? Why else would I live this wretched life, but that long ago I was sworn to Chameol and fell from her favor? All my life is now come to this: to win back what I once lost through cowardice and folly. And now I have found the means to do it. Have you never noticed the tent neither Ulfra nor Nix nor any of that pack will go near? The rats don't gnaw at the tent pole, and the moths leave the canvas alone. If you've a nose for smells of the inhuman kind—and eating fire has that effect on the sinuses—it reeks."

"Of Otherworld?"

Pyle shook his head, sober himself. "Of evil."

The Badger woke to a strange noise, and slowly came to recognize it as scissors on paper. When he opened his eyes, he found it was Nix, sitting cross-legged in the middle of the tent, cutting out masks.

"That's quite a pile of masks you have there. Couldn't you sleep?"

Nix shook his head and held his handiwork up to his face. The first mask, hardly surprisingly, was a wolf with bared fangs and a lolling tongue. "Grrrrrrrrrrr!" said Nix.

The Badger allowed himself to be rent limb from limb. "Very nice. And this one?"

The second turned out to be the woman from the tattoo, each eel in her hairstyle cut out individually and fixed in a slot so that by pulling on a thread Nix could make them writhe very well. For all its mechanical ingenuity and vivid coloring, the Badger only shuddered and said nothing to praise it.

This mask held a surprise, however: a face painted on the

reverse, framed not with living eels but with hair of jet shot with indigo. It was a pity the boy was not at court, the Badger thought. He had a future as a portrait painter.

Nix moved a paper strip in its groove, and the eyes in the mask changed color, from twins of icy blue to a mismatched pair of blue and green. The lady held the Badger's gaze with her own changeable one and planted on his cheek a paper kiss.

"And what of this last one, the one you were working on, Nix?"

It was a demon, a monster. More than that, it was an evil intelligence: a face seamed with veins and scars, the lip cleft, the tongue in the mouth purple as a serpent's. The Badger stared at it with the horror not of nightmare but of recognition. He tore it from the boy's face and cast it into the fire.

Nix watched it curl to a lace of embers and ash. He sighed the stuttering sigh of a child exhausted by its own crying, even though his eyes were dry. Then he crawled into the Badger's lap and buried his small snowy head under the Badger's chin.

The Badger rocked the boy until he felt Nix's breathing lapse into the easy canter of sleep. Still holding the sleeping boy, he wandered around the tent, lighting lamps and muttering all the old childhood prayers he could remember, until, closer to dawn than to midnight, Elric returned to the tent.

The Badger dreamed.

He was in a prison cell, and Nix was at the grate in the street. The Badger of the dream passed something through the bars into Nix's small hand: two marbles, one green and one blue.

"Find her."

He woke and found Ulfra standing over him, gazing down at Nix where he slept, curled up in a blanket like a motherless puppy, at the foot of the Badger's cot. She bent to nuzzle the snowy hair, take the boy's pulse behind his ear with her kiss. Her look to the Badger said, Just this once. Then she was gone.

Find her, echoed the dream in his brain. But was it a dream, after all, or a memory?

In the kitchen tent, the cook was composing a strange salad. She had gone to the town in the afternoon and stolen some greens from walled gardens; the rest of her medley she had plucked from the roadside as she made her way back to Folderol's camp.

"Here's rocket, for deceit, and moon-ruled purslane," the old woman recited, tearing the greenery between her hands. "And basil for spite and grief-struck marigold. Yes, this will do me very well." Then she dressed it all with oil and wormwood vinegar and set it by under a damp cloth to keep fresh while she prepared the rest of the meal.

The crow looked down from where it was steaming its feathers above the sighing kettle and murmured something that sounded like, "Pity, have pity-pity!" The cat wound round the cook's ankles, mewling a song of ruthlessness and begging for giblets.

At lunch the Badger leaned over and peered jealously at Pyle's plate.

"Salad! Where did you get *salad*?"

Pyle winked at Grisaudra and kept forking the lightly oiled greenery into his mouth. A dish covered with a towel had appeared outside his tent with a note in a womanly hand: *Here is something more wholesome than anything to come out of the kitchen. From one who wishes you well.* Who but the herbwoman would have done such a thing? He would have to ask her what she had dressed it with: the flavor teased his tongue, its name just out of reach.

The Badger fished in his pockets. "Here, man—a half-silver for a bite of that. What do you say?"

The fire-eater's only answer was to throw back his head and plunge his fork, wrapped with the last leaf of rocket, halfway down his throat, as if swallowing a sword.

Grisaudra was puzzled. Why had he winked? She certainly knew too much about herbs to jumble them together in dangerous juxtapositions in a salad. Well, if people wanted to traipse through the countryside and graze on medicinals like a flock of sheep, Grisaudra supposed they would have to live with the consequences. She herself would rather have eaten fire, or worse, than rocket and marigold and basil together.

The hour before the first performance found Elric transforming himself into the duchess and the Badger tying bells to the horses' harnesses when a loud commotion erupted outside.

The troupe had gathered at the point where the river flowed closest the camp. A figure could be seen struggling in the strong current.

Grisaudra was standing apart from the rest, with Ulfra and Nix, when they came up.

"Who is it?"

"Pyle—"

"What happened?"

"He ran past, screaming and beating at his clothes, as though he were on fire, but there wasn't a spark—"

The Badger dove into the water and fought to free the

fire-eater from the deadly river; like a ravenous giant, the river had been known to swallow barges and herds of cattle whole. Twice he had him, only to have the stronger pull of the river wrench the limp form from his grasp. Then Pyle was gone, and he himself was a prisoner of the water's grip.

And suddenly the Badger was battling the water for possession of his own memory. It was as if he struggled to break the cold and numbing embrace of a sorceress, the eels roping around his neck like a noose. In some watery pool, her captive, the beauty from the other side of Nix's mask, called out to him, a plea for help or a warning.

"No—let her go!" The Badger tried to cry out, but the river rushed into his mouth and silenced him. The enchantress drew a heavy dark curtain of water over his head, and he was swallowed by a great blackness, through which a blinding white light seemed to split his skull. Before the water hurtled him into unconsciousness, the Badger saw the two faces merge and melt into one, saw the evil face swallowed up in and consumed by the beauty of the other. As his lungs filled with a great breath of the river, the Badger knew there was only one woman and that evil knew no part of her.

They fished the Badger out of the river on the end of a pruning hook; of Pyle there was no longer any sign. The Badger was at first more dead than alive, but by the time most of the water had been pumped out of him the living half had gained the upper hand. He opened his eyes, which focused neither on Elric nor Grisaudra, who were bending near, but on Ulfra. He spat river and spoke.

"Caitlin," he said.

Serpentine

Ylfcwen sat up in bed, snapping her wings open and shut while she thought. *Snap. Snap. Snap.* It was a terrible habit, of which her mother had tried with every ruse to break her. *You'll tear them right off if you keep that up!* Ylfcwen began to chew a thumbnail instead.

At last the elf queen rose and went to the wall covered with a living tapestry of violets. She parted the leaves to reveal a silver mirror black with tarnish. Ylfcwen breathed on the mirror to mist it, then knelt before it.

"Liege Drusian, I beg audience with you."

"Yes, daughter."

"The changeling we sent Above will die soon."

"As it must be with all goblins in the realm of men, once the substitution has been discovered."

Ylfcwen bit her lip. "But only if the human child remains with me. You have claimed this—this bram for yourself. What am I to get out of the bargain?"

"You did not cherish this goblin when you dispatched Ordella to effect the deception."

"No. One does not *cherish* a goblin, exactly. But one does not like to *waste* them."

The mirror went black, and the leaves and heads of the violets curled toward it to conceal it again, indicating that this audience was at an end.

"Liege Drusian."

The mirror lightened a little, and the violets appeared to lift their heads.

"I would like permission to go Above."

"To what end?"

"To bring back what is mine."

Though Caitlin and Newt did not consult it on the matter, the court etiquette had this to say on royal excursions to the realms of light and air.

Going Above

Members of court, when receiving a special dispensation to venture Above, must go forth dressed as if banished, in clothes the color of earth, though for the queen herself leaf green is permissible. To venture forth in full court dress of elven silk is not only ostentatious but dangerous, unless one wishes to live out the balance of one's allotted ten score and twenty as a sideshow or lap pet. Only two elf queens have ever been known to venture to the surface. Ygwynyd, having banished her human lover, was astonished to find she loved him and went to dwell with him as a human woman. The infamous Yvyola abandoned the court out of boredom and was last sighted running an inn on the coast near Chameol, where she lived under the name of Emma.

Ylfcwen settled on a suit of loam-colored fur, a cane, and round green spectacles; with her strange opal eyes she felt it wisest to move in the human world as a blind beggar woman. It would be a most useful disguise for, posing as one unseeing, she might move in the mortal world almost unseen.

Ylfcwen searched her mother's trinket box for some old silver coins, which she ordered melted down and reminted after the current fashion. She removed from her ivory hands all her jeweled rings and elvish seals of state and hung them from her waist in an old goatskin purse along with the coins. Then Ylfcwen stood back and laughed at herself in the looking glass.

"Yes, we have long fancied the idea of a holiday on Chameol!"

Cerulean's directions brought Newt and Caitlin through a maze of side tunnels, and the stone walls on either side gradually changed hue, from deepest sapphire through a myriad of teals and aquamarines to the brilliant green of serpentine. Newt clambered from his napping place in Caitlin's pocket to her shoulder, where he bit her hard enough behind the ear to break the skin.

"Ow!" She put up a hand to the bite, which had already gone warmly pins and needles. "What was that for?"

"A little preventative. There are things here that will bite you with a far worse effect."

"Vipers?"

"Among other things." Newt did not elaborate on what these were, leaving Caitlin to conjure them in her own mind in dreadful variety.

It appeared that Serpentine, unlike Pj'aurinoor and Cerulean, did not boast a lofty chamber. Rather, the passage in front of them was suddenly honeycombed green rock, a maze of boxwood hedges turned to stone by some enchantment. Caitlin could not help but remember another maze and roses in the snow at Ninthstile. The memory of that brush with evil made her shudder.

Courage, Newt's mind murmured into her own. *You will need it here.*

Cerulean's odd words came back to her: "Do not go forward or backward, left or right, but in the one direction you think you cannot go, for that is the only safe way." There were forks in the tunnel to her left and right and a wall of green stone straight ahead. Caitlin walked straight ahead, and as she neared the wall, it suddenly was no longer made of stone but of living vipers, poised to strike. With her next footstep the vipers changed to stout briar branches, forming a solid wall of thorns, embedded with the armor of heroes lost in the attempt to cut through it. Caitlin was not a foot away when the wall shifted for the third time and became a barrier of white-hot steel. In the blast of heat Caitlin felt her eyelashes singe, and her tongue and eyes seemed on fire, leaving her mute and blind. "Nothing is as it seems," Cerulean's voice said in her mind. Blindly, Caitlin stepped forward into the white heat.

The wall vanished at her touch like mist, and she was facing another fork in the tunnel, with three choices this time instead of two. Behind her there was suddenly a wall and seemingly no return from the way she had come.

Why was it everything suddenly reminded her of something from the past? The maze at Ninthstile, the chamber of the dragon Ormr, and now the catacombs known as the Devil's Sieve.

Maybe that is the real weapon, Caitlin thought. *To keep me lost in a maze of my own memories, of places I was once, so I can't keep my mind on where I am now.* "Newt, I am going to close my eyes, and you must dowse my way for me."

"Do you think it wise to enter Serpentine's lair with your eyes closed?"

"Maybe not the wisest way, but it seems to me the only way."

"All right, then. Forward."

But simply closing her eyes was not enough to outwit the hallucinations. With her first step Caitlin felt herself slip from a cliff's edge and plummet through space. Newt's voice in her ear next steered her to the right, and her feet seemed to sink into the deadly ooze of a bog. The salamander then guided her around a bit of hanging rock.

"Duck your head," Newt said. "That's it. Now go to your left. . . ."

But before Caitlin could move, a voice, silky and sibilant, coiled around her in the darkness.

"If you please, watch where you step."

Caitlin opened her eyes to look full into the unblinking gaze of a pair of small black eyes. These were set rather too far apart to be human, in a long, flat head covered with jewellike scales. Two pinholes marked the nose; the mouth was wide and lipless. Of ears there was no evidence. The body itself took a more human shape, though there was a superfluity of arms, and the torso was covered with emerald scales. The lower half was draped in a voluminous robe of silk, the whole creature propped up on a heap of cushions brocaded in green-and-gold silk.

They had apparently interrupted a meal. Caitlin caught sight of a dish of quails' eggs before Serpentine drew a cloth over the rest.

"You will excuse me if I don't offer you any. For some reason, humans find my diet repulsive."

"Don't stop on my account. I doubt I would find it so. I have had to eat strange things myself out of necessity."

"That is kind of you, but then, you did not see what was in the other dishes." One of the arms beckoned Caitlin to a seat among the cushions, then offered a dish of pickled hummingbirds' eggs. When these were refused, Serpentine took one herself. "You intrigue me no little amount. No one has ever ventured so far into my lair, not even a seer."

"Not even Drusian?"

The glittering dark eyes betrayed no surprise. "No, Drusian would not honor me in such a manner. When I have a need, I solicit an audience. My needs have been few; we have a long and honorable understanding, Drusian and I."

"You both deal in death."

"No, in sleep and in desire and in dreams. You know the tales? Some are just that: only tales; but a surprising number are true. You are a seer; you know the ancient ones used dream adders to induce their oracular trances. I have been worshipped in ages past, in times far distant, by races whose names would mean nothing to you. But no longer. The greatest boons I have granted these five hundred years have been sleep for the dying, peaceful dreams for the mad, a cordial for the lovesick."

"A deadly cordial for something so fleeting as desire."

"Love may be fleeting, but that makes the desire of the moment no less powerful. The lover will give anything to win her object. What is the risk, when compared with the end?"

"Love can be won, surely, through other means than using venom to enslave the heart."

"Perhaps it eases the lover's ache as much as it relieves the invalid's pain or the madman's delirium."

Caitlin could not answer. She had needed such a venom, or something like it, herself, that first night alone on Chameol, when she thought grief and misgiving and love would surely kill her.

"But it would not avail me now," she said at last. "There is nothing among your rare drugs to ease this ache. It's love that is paining me, though I dare say I will be ill and mad before it is through with me."

The small dark eyes fixed on her contemplatively. "What sort of loss is it that grieves you?"

"That of a child vanished."

Serpentine nodded. "Yes, you feel these things more keenly, having your offspring one or two at a time. If you had them in broods, you might not miss one so much."

Serpentine shifted on her pillows and adjusted her silken robe, trying to make herself comfortable and realizing true comfort in her present situation was impossible. "Do you have an idea who has taken your child?"

"Drusian himself."

The black eyes glittered. "Himself? Are you so sure of that?"

"I know Ylfcwen sent a serving-woman to fetch my son away, and Ylfcwen serves none but Drusian."

"But you seem so certain it was at the master's bidding. Has it never occurred to you that it might have been Iiliana who ordered it?"

"Iiliana!"

"Who else had your trust? Who else the opportunity and the authority to order it?"

"But what reason could she have had?"

"You might better ask which reason of a thousand. A child must always claim you above all other oaths and allegiances. A son might become a weapon against Chameol, a pawn to sway you toward Myrrhlock and the other side. And simply in himself, Bram must diminish that part of yourself that you could give over to serve Chameol and serve Iiliana."

Caitlin's mind spun with images: Iiliana bending over the cradle, Iiliana telling her Ordella had gone. "No—"

"No? Very well. I will not mention the other explanation."

"What do you mean?"

"That Bram is not your son."

Caitlin laughed. "That is impossible!"

"Is it? Hear me, otherworld daughter. Bram is the child they put into your arms, but Grimald is the son you gave life. Remember the Badger's words: *Mooncalves breed only mooncalves.* What other sort of son could he father, the product of an unnatural union himself? The tanner's daughter's son, and the tanner's son—"

Caitlin looked into Serpentine's eyes. "So! Is *that* your

game? Taking my own fears and feeding them, then reciting them back to me? You take an inchworm of suspicion and turn it into a serpent of fear run mad. My fears become your weapon against me."

Serpentine shifted her weight, adjusting the robe. "I hope you have no idea of my interceding on your behalf with the master. My sense of courtesy, as well as the understanding between us, would prevent it."

"All I desire is safe passage to his chamber, where I can plead my case."

Serpentine gestured with an emerald hand. "It is not in my power to prevent you. You will excuse my not showing you out? I am sitting on my brood, and I expect they will begin to hatch quite shortly. Do watch where you step."

Fiddle and Pomamber lay sprawled in the pantry, the youth's head pillowed on the mastiff's shaggy flank. Fiddle's hand trailed in a bowl of gooseberries and cream, and Pomamber's jaws were closed around the bone from a joint of mutton. They were surrounded by the other litter of their repast: crusts from a number of custard tarts, a rope of sausages liberated from its hook, emptied pots of jam, the ruin of a meat pie. The dog and boy were not so much alseep as sated into a stupor.

Pomamber woke first, and her altered breathing woke the boy. They both sniffed the air, both caught the scent that said first "stranger" and then said "otherworld." Cautiously, Fiddle lifted the latch on the pantry door and the pair padded on silent feet down the deserted hallway, hoping they would find the otherworldly intruder before it found them.

Ylfcwen had come not by boat but by way of the tunnel beneath the Strait of Chameol itself, a passageway so ancient

Ylfcwen's own surveys placed it on the other side of the island entirely. The trapdoor had not opened on daylight in a good five hundred years; at last, lying on her back in the tunnel and giving it a solid kick with both feet at once, Ylfcwen was able to break the corroded hinges. She found herself in the grape arbor of the garden below Caitlin's bedroom window, eye to eye with a raven.

She settled her claim to the grape arbor by throwing a slipper at the raven. When she had dusted herself off a bit, Ylfcwen looked around, thinking the mortal race knew little enough about the art of horticulture. That ridiculous fish pond, with its dreadful fountain! Those tousled vines were badly in need of restraint, and the shaggy beds of lamb's ear wanted a firm hand with the pruning shears. How anyone could think to put those roses in that spot was more than Ylfcwen could imagine. They might *survive* there, but certainly they could never *thrive*. She raised her glance from the neglected rosebush to the walls of the palace, feeling a strange and unaccustomed pang. If such was their husbandry of flowers, what could they be expected to do with a goblin, which was as thorny but no less delicate in its way?

She made her way first to the chamber where the mirror-Caitlin lay sleeping. It was in that chamber that the smell of goblin lay heaviest. Ylfcwen kneeled by the empty basket in the alcove and swept up some crumbs the pigeons had missed. Macaroons! Had she fed him macaroons? If she had, it was bad, very bad. How much further it might have gone, Ylfcwen hated to think. It was a bad enough sign that the scent of goblin was strongest in a room where the goblin wasn't.

A quick survey of the rooms told her the whole household was asleep. This was not a charm of Ordella's making, Ylfcwen knew. When a changeling was exchanged for a human child, no charm was necessary any stronger than a raven's feather hung by a red thread from an eastern rafter to keep the dogs from barking. Such a deep sleep as Ylfcwen now observed was another matter entirely. It was not just about a simple exchanging of a goblin for a baby, no; it presaged the awakening of one who had slept a far more ancient sleep. Looking about her at the bodies of the sleepers, Ylfcwen shivered, remembering a passage from her elvish catechism:

> In that time the slumbering world shall waken, and the waking world shall be cast into a great sleep, and the doorway between the one world and the other shall be closed forevermore, and none shall thereafter pass between them. For in those days the royal exile shall end, the ancient court shall rise once more from its biding-place, and all present things shall be banished, and all things known overthrown.

Ylfcwen knitted her brow, pondering the possibility of an extended visit in the mortal world.

When she entered Iiliana's chamber and saw the goblin lying asleep, Ylfcwen felt her heart sink. She had only to pinch him awake and look into his yellow eyes to know the worst. He had been fed macaroons and nursed at the breast, and rocked and lullabied and dandled on the knee, no doubt. Even all that would not have been enough to make Ylfcwen abandon hope; he might have been rehabilitated, in time. But from the look in the yellow eyes she knew she was too late. Even in a short space of time they had named him and begun to love him, and now he was more human than goblin. A human child could be dosed with drops and catechized and brought along with a mild mixture of nectar and root wine. But once a goblin child had known human love, it was no use trying to get it back. A goblin enlightened, or "brought to air," as the saying went, could see through the enchantments of the Otherworld and could not be made to work at the looms of the court or the mines of the gemfields. They sooner or later went mad or died in a most troublesome fashion.

The elf queen went out into the hallway feeling light-headed. Light poisoning, probably. She would find a dark closet and close her eyes and take a sip from the flask of root wine she had brought with her.

To her astonishment, the door of the first linen closet she tried opened to reveal a frightened boy and a large dog, quaking beneath an eiderdown. To Fiddle, who had been expecting a demon, the sight of Ylfcwen was still unsettling; with her dark spectacles and strange fur garments, she was like one of the blind mice from the nursery rhyme, come looking with a carving knife for the thief who had robbed her pantry.

Ylfcwen removed her spectacles to look at her prize more closely. Fiddle was a good height and practically grown into a man of the size and variety the elf queen most favored. This would make up a little for the loss of the goblin baby. In a year or two, he could begin his studies of the court etiquette and the elvish tongues, and by his seventh year in the Otherworld he might even sit for the examination to become her consort, if she hadn't tired of him by then.

Fiddle stood transfixed by the smooth opal gaze, seeing in the rose-and-green fire of its depths the fulfillment of every vague yearning, feeling the same way he felt at the moment of waking from a particularly pleasant dream. Looking into the elf queen's eyes, Fiddle even began to think that his waking life must be illusory and the life of dreams the true existence. The opal eyes said this was indeed so. She was holding out her hand, and in it there was the silver jigger cap of the pocket flask, full of something heady and bitter, something Fiddle knew he shouldn't drink.

Pomamber, who had been standing whimpering and quaking with fear, took this opportunity to bolt. This roused

Fiddle to his senses again, and he pelted out of the linen closet after the mastiff as if all the demons of the Otherworld were after him.

Ylfcwen sighed. "These mortals! Why do I trouble with them? One might as well tie a napkin on a jackrabbit and teach it to eat lettuce with a fork."

It seemed a shame to have made the journey and have to return so soon with nothing to show for her trouble, so Ylfcwen resolved to see as much of the country Above as she could, just in case it turned out to be her only visit. She found a boat tied up in a hidden harbor, a pretty, light craft just the right size and color for her, tugging at its moorings like a high-spirited greyhound eager to be off. Ylfcwen settled her cane and bundle in one end and arranged herself at the other.

"Take me to the nearest landfall," she commanded.

The boat obeyed.

At the first turning Caitlin was lost again in the windings of the tunnels and would not have been able to swear to the direction from which she had come.

Newt twisted a lock of hair near Caitlin's ear; he did this, she had found, when he was thinking.

"I was wondering that, too," she said.

"All right, thought reader. Tell me what I was wondering."

"Why Serpentine let us off so easily. And where were all these vipers you were so worried about?"

"As for the one, she was busied with her brood. And as for the others, it seems we are to be allowed to pass unharmed. For the vipers answer to Serpentine, and she answers to Drusian."

"Well, I wonder when we will come to these doors. We've

had steel and fire and vipers' heads already. What possibly can be left, I can't imagine."

"Eldrin of Tenthmoon."

"Who was he?"

"A king. He craved power over past, present, and future, so at his bidding his court magician built him a cabinet of yew. It had three doors, one of which opened into the past, one on the present, and the third on the future."

"And where did his cabinet take him?"

"Well, the chamber had a flaw in its design, or the magician had a sense of humor that the king did not appreciate, for there was no telling which of the doors of the cabinet opened on which aspect. The king, in his displeasure, turned the magician out of his house, but he could not bring himself to destroy the cabinet. He locked it in a tower room, thinking that someday he might discover its mystery."

"Don't tell me. The king has three daughters, and each in turn stumbles upon the forbidden room. The eldest vanishes into the past, the next-to-eldest into the future, so the youngest returns to the present unknown to her own father, and she is married off to a swineherd."

"You would have made a good storyteller."

"Am I right, then?"

"In most particulars. The eldest was sent back five hundred years and became a wealthy spice trader. The middle one was sent forward only about fifty years and had to live out her life as a widow without ever having known her husband or much else of life. The youngest was returned unknown to the father, but she was not married off to a swineherd. When a strange young woman appeared in his court, claiming to be his daughter, the king ordered her imprisoned in the tower room."

"And what happened to her?"

"Oh, she lived out her life there, unable to decide whether the fate that awaited her through any of the doors would improve upon the one known to her, however dreary."

Caitlin had paused on a threshold once before. Through the first door a life had awaited her on Chameol fulfilling her seer's gifts, in which she might remember the Badger but live ever apart from him. Through the second door lay a life as an ordinary woman, her otherworld sight stripped from her, with no memory of Chameol or the Badger.

But now that she had made her choice and passed through the first door, not even the consolation of Bram was to be allowed her. Caitlin was more certain than ever now that the Master ruled not only sleep and dreams and desires but death itself, and that with every lost hour her chances of reclaiming her son dwindled. She saw them as the canary orchid, wilting and dimming in the dark, and it was not only Bram she was losing; it was love and light itself. Her life would be spent on Chameol as its seer, higher in rank even than Iiliana, with all the mysteries of the ancient runebooks to solve. In her mind, Caitlin saw herself as an old woman, bent over a dusty tome, alone in a tower room. She was the image of her old guardian, Abagtha, gnarled and twisted like an old tree in the wind, bleached grey.

No, thought Caitlin, she would return to the sea and live her life out neither as Caitlin the woman nor Caitlin the seer, but as some third creature, beyond speech, lulled in the heavy sighing of the billows.

"Yes," she said suddenly. "There must be a *third* door." A way to live not in the past or in the future but in the present.

Something fell to the stones paving the tunnel. It was Newt, suddenly glass again. He had brought her as far as he could bring her. Caitlin slipped the glass salamander into her pocket. With the next step the light of the canary orchid guttered as if in a strong gust and went out.

"All right!" she said to the darkness. "What will satisfy you? You have everything of mine. You have taken my son, denied me my only guide and companion, even extinguished my light. Well, I have half of my reason left and nearly all my wits. We'll see how far they can take me in the dark before you claim them, too."

In the chamber the crystal book swirled with illegible words, ink and oil in water, forming and reforming but never quite taking shape. Amidst the cryptic, changeable runes, pictures formed briefly on the crystal leaves. There appeared in turn a woman who might have been Caitlin or Ulfra, a smaller bent figure that might have been Grisaudra or Ordella, a baby that might have been a goblin. Then the translucent pages dimmed and went blank.

A ghostly hand moved a piece on the game board from a region inlaid with green stone to a golden circle in the center.

Bram stirred under the blanket of ravens' feathers and cried weakly. The hand reached out and gently smoothed the dark hair. The child gazed into eyes that seemed to hold all the light in the world captive in their orbs; the sight calmed him, and he reached out with a chubby hand to touch the bright rings: one of tiger's eye, one of sapphire, and one of serpentine. Bram was lifted from his cradle and held up so he could see the pictures take shape on the pages of the crystal book.

A voice roused the stillness in the chamber, the wind singing of light in a cave that had never known the sun.

"Hush, sweetling. Look, here is your mother, come for you. It will not be long now."

THIRTEEN

The Snake Charmer

*T*he arrangement would have suited Folderol perfectly, if it had not been for the snakes. In all other respects, Hessie would have made an admirable Mistress Folderol. She was well-featured, even-tempered, no more voluptuous than was becoming, and a good manager of money. If she had been anything but the troupe's snake charmer, he would have made her his wife at the first opportunity. But the old rogue's imagination conjured too many serpents—sleeping in his boot toes, basking among the cushions in his favorite chair—to make the idea completely attractive.

Hessie privately thought it was just as well that she made her living the way she did, for she was not at all certain being Mistress Folderol would have agreed with her. But for all that he was a foolish, vain, thieving kind of man, toward Hessie herself the old rogue was generous, affectionate, and flattering in the right proportion. She might have had a younger man with better teeth, but would a younger man have massaged her feet after a long day? Whenever Folderol tried her patience, she had only to tweak his beard and tease that she would turn him into a snake.

"Oh ho, turn me into a snake, she says. Ha, ha!"

"Well," she would say with a shrug, "how do you think I tamed all these others?"

Hessie took great pride in the fact that she used none of the customary snake charmer's ruses in her performance.

The fangs of her adders were intact and had not been plugged with wax. Neither were their jaws sewn shut, and the poison glands had not been cut out or tied off. Hessie relied instead on the curious docility of snakes in captivity and the occasional saucer of milk laced with laudanum.

Their morning and evening feedings had come to coincide with the donning and doffing of their mistress's professional costume, including a gilt headdress and matching fingernails, which together lent an aura of mystery with just the right touch of the sinister. Hessie sat at her dressing table now, dissolving the spirit gum that held the gold talons in place and talking to the snakes, a habit she had fallen into almost without realizing it. The largest and oldest adder, Arabella, already fed, had coiled herself gently around Hessie's throat, apparently intent on the process of talon removal.

"Sybella, don't be so greedy. Give your brother a chance. Oliver, you mustn't be so timid; you'll starve to death if you wait your turn that way. Which do you think I should have made up, Arabella, the olive or the lavender?" Hessie's old confidante, the leopard-woman, had been by with sketches and swatches for Hessie's new costumes, a present Hessie insisted that Folderol had promised her. And didn't she deserve it?

"The trouble with the olive is, while it sets *you* off well, Arabella, it makes *me* look sallow. Perhaps if I wore a scarf of some other color nearer my face it would offset it a little. That crimson silk, perhaps. Yes, that might answer very well."

Hessie had been on an errand to the kitchen tent to fetch milk for the snakes when she first sensed something was awry. It wasn't just that the milk the woman had given her was sour and Hessie had finally had to buy her milk from an obliging farm woman who had an equally obliging cow.

No, it was the cat, the strange harlequin cat that spurned milk and catnip and mice and seemed to take its only pleasure in tormenting that poor crow. Something was very wrong with that cat, Hessie was sure.

Folderol had only laughed. "Nothing wrong with it—it doesn't care for the necklace you wear, is all."

"Arabella was back in my tent, having a nap. There is something very wrong with that cook, too, I tell you."

"Well, I can't fire her. She's worked for me—" Folderol tugged his calico beard a moment in consternation. "I can't remember how long, but long enough anyway."

Hessie couldn't remember when the woman had come to cook for the troupe. She seemed to think there had been someone else quite recently, but the face and name of that other cook seemed to have been erased somehow from her mind. Surely, her memory wasn't *that* bad? Then the present sullen woman must have been there as long as Hessie had— mustn't she?

The leopard-woman came, and Hessie told her to make up the olive with a crimson trim. Soon Hessie found herself standing on a stool, cradling a bolt of silk in her arms, its train wound about her like a cocoon.

"Tell me, Tansy, who was the cook when you were here?"

The leopard-woman looked up, her muzzle abristle with pins as if with whiskers. "Have you been drinking some of that milk you give your snakes? Who was the cook when I was here, she asks! Why, can you have forgotten our dear Toby?"

Coil by coil, something deep within the snake charmer's memory stirred: the kindly knife thrower who had one day lost his courage and had to put his talent with cutlery to another purpose. "Toby! Of course—how could I ever have forgotten him?"

"I can't imagine. Oh, Hessie, he used to make old Feather-All so jealous, the way he fed you like a pet."

"His hash and eggs. What I wouldn't give for the man's hash and eggs. I don't even remember him leaving, Tansy. Where did Toby go?"

"Well, he left after I went to set up the shop. I only heard about it when I ran into him later. He said it was the oddest thing, that he had gone into the kitchen tent one morning and found a strange woman there—strange-foreign and strange-peculiar—and when he went to complain, old Folly-and-Brawl told him he didn't know what he was talking about, that the woman had been with him for years. Now, *there's* someone who doctors his saucer of milk in the evening."

Hessie thought nothing, not even the better part of a barrel of stout, could have made Folderol sack his old friend Toby. How could they both—they and all the rest of the troupe—have forgotten him so easily? And what had possessed Folderol to hire that dour old woman, with her pressed-leek soups and cinder-coated chickens?

The candle had burned until the flame finally drowned in its own wax. It was light, then, anyway. The Badger stretched and pushed back his chair; he would have set down his pencil, worn now to a stub, but his hand was cramped around it, and he could not let it go.

The tabletop in front of him was littered with drawings, sheets covered front and back with dozens of small sketches, Caitlin over and over, as his mind's eye was now able to recall her: standing in a market square, wearing a collar of bells; sprawled in a corridor in a billowing silk dress with a litter of kittens in her lap; stooping in the curling shallow foam of the moonlit sea; Caitlin having her hair cut off by the old eel-seller, the eel-seller who had been Elric in disguise. All night he had scrawled in a desperate haste, lest his memory should leave him again in an hour. Now that the danger seemed safely past, he could use a shave and a bath.

The tapping of the razor on the edge of the basin woke Elric, who had fallen asleep a little before dawn, assured by then that the Badger's frantic scribbling was a sign of further mending, not further mischief. By the time Elric had bathed as well, the drawings had been put away, and the Badger had begun to fill a fresh sheet with his stable shorthand of a monk's script.

"Take a rest, man. Think of your eyes, if you won't have pity on your body or your brain."

The Badger put out his lower lip and blew a shock of hair out of his eyes. "I'm all right. It's just that we've wasted so much time, and we don't know much more than we knew the day we went to see the shoemaker." He crumpled the paper and raised his arm to throw it into the fire, but Elric took it from him and smoothed it out on the table to read it. The Badger had drawn two overlapping circles, one labeled "Oncemoon" and one labeled "Folderol's T." In the first circle he had written the names of the mad and missing in Oncemoon: Tilda and her father, the shoemaker; the mayor; and the merchant. In the other circle he had written the names of Hodge and Pyle. Where the circles overlapped, the Badger had written his own name.

Elric glanced at the younger knight sharply. "Why your name?"

The Badger's eyes were bright with sleeplessness or dread. "Think about it: I'm the only thing that links the two sets of events."

Elric shook his head and took the pencil from the Badger, or what was left of the pencil; while he spoke, the Badger had been whittling it with his knife, and it was now not much more than a splinter. Without a word, Elric added a name to the space where the circles met.

The Badger frowned. "Grisaudra? But she hasn't been touched by the malady."

"Hasn't she?" Elric was thinking of the look he had seen in her eyes that day he had been coming out of the kitchen tent with matches. "Come, Badger. It's high time we had a talk with Grisaudra."

The flames had nearly consumed the cap of owl's feathers; the marked tarot deck and the wooden dice were already ashes. The contents of all her vials and bottles had been emptied into the river. Now the same icy water that had shocked the Badger into memory dyed the dreams of pike and perch and trout all the colors of a wizard's paint box. Her catmint and juniper cordial had gone as well, for it might have deadened her pain, and Grisaudra wanted to feel anguish in each fresh variety it presented.

All hope had vanished with that one word: *Caitlin.* But that one word had done far more than dash her hopes: It had opened her eyes to the nature and extent of her own folly. She stood in front of the mirror, forcing herself to gaze on her reflection there. Her eye and scar now appeared as more than a disfigurement of nature; they seemed to her the outward sign of a disfigured soul. It was not the Badger's eyes that haunted her now, but Elric's, as cold, grey, and unforgiving as steel.

Self-loathing is a bitter medicine, and too great a dose can work greater evil than it cures. At last Grisaudra turned away from the mirror and began to place in her pockets those few things she had brought with her from Oncemoon. She had only meant to travel with the Badger until his memory could be returned, and while she doubted his "hauntings" would ever really cease, Grisaudra saw nothing to be gained in staying another hour among the troupe.

As she belted her tunic of chain mail about her once more, she was girding her spirit as well for her return to the marsh. Back in her hut with the cat and the pigs, Grisaudra wished she could be certain of banishing from her mind not only the Badger but Elric as well. His face—and the look of horror the accidental dose of drops had brought to it—had begun to haunt her sleep and to frequent her more familiar nightmares. Suddenly the mocking face of the handsome young soldier was his; the shroud maker leered with those grey eyes, and it was Elric who wielded the sword as it swung toward her, singing of steely death. It was the look in the eyes that woke her, a look that said he believed the worst of her. If he thought such dire things about her now, what would he think if he knew the whole of it? And what, Grisaudra asked herself crossly, does his good opinion mean to you? He is a wormwood kind of man, six pints of bile and bitterness sewn up in a human hide. But the truth of it was that somehow his good opinion had come to mean a great deal, and the more he distrusted her the more Grisaudra longed to gain his trust. *Caitlin:* That one word had wakened something else than shame in her; it had killed one hope but had brought to life a hope of another sort.

To cure herself of this way of thinking, Grisaudra removed from her pockets the charms Elric had tied to her fortune-teller's getup. In the fire, the small green glove curled into a fist in the flames, grasping at ashes. The faces on the playing cards grew beards of fire until finally the features were lost in flame.

She would fill her pockets with things harmless in their usefulness, incapable of rousing her to memory or dreams. A slice of cold pigeon pie, some cheese, a bit of bread. The bread was moldy, and it was as she held it in her hand, poised to throw it away, that Grisaudra was struck by a thought so startling and overpowering that she gasped and sat, staring at the green crust in her hand.

"Of course—of course! But that means—oh, I must tell Elric!"

The scream of the harlequin cat nearly made her jump out of her skin. It arched its back in the opening of her tent, hissing and yowling with a sound that made Grisaudra shudder.

"You hideous thing!" She stood with a shoe in her hand but could not bring herself to throw it. "Grisaudra!" she said sternly to herself. "Surely, you're not afraid of that cat!"

Instantly, she knew she was greatly afraid of it indeed. She held the shoe tightly against her chest and began to back away, feeling behind her for a willow switch, her walking stick, for anything. Her hand closed not on a stick, but on something sleek and feathered. She spun about, frightening the crow out of its wits, so that the one shrieked and the other croaked in fright. Without knowing why, Grisaudra dropped the shoe and clutched the bird to her. Its beak hung open with fright and it shuddered in her arms. Grisaudra held it tightly in front of her, as if it were a charm against the cat.

"Let it go." The hooded figure in the shadow of the tent flap was the wrong height for the cook, though the voice was not unlike hers. Grisaudra blinked and rubbed her eyes with the back of one hand; the figure before her seemed to shimmer and change. Surely it was taller. It drew closer and in a different voice spoke again. "Let it go, Grisaudra of Oncemoon, and the prize I promised you can still be yours."

Her heart was beating as fast as the bird's, but her voice came calmly enough when called. "No, thank you. It seemed a bad bargain when I thought about it: a husband with a brain so addled he could think *me* a beauty."

"It would be as I showed you: You would be beautiful and he would love you."

"No. Being in thrall is rather different from being in love, I think."

"It is Caitlin who has enthralled him, but he will recover

from it. But will you surrender him to her so easily, Grisaudra, if I tell you she is dead?"

Grisaudra sank slowly to the floor. The crow in her arms gave out a strange human moan. "She can't be . . ."

"She is dead, or as good as dead. If she does not lose her life, she will certainly lose her reason. She will not be the first seer to go mad; there is an asylumful in Tenthmoon."

He had come up to her as he spoke, and as he took the crow from her arms his hood fell back. He was Myrrhlock, not the old Necromancer with the seamed skull and harelip and terrible eyes, but Myrrhlock as he must have been before pride and will were twisted into something old and evil. This was a flawless face, perfect in proportion and shape; only its utter coldness kept it from being wholly beautiful. The strange, mercurial eyes compensated for this lack; their magnetic gaze made it impossible for Grisaudra to look away. In his arms the crow seemed barely to breathe, its eyes nearly shut.

Myrrhlock cupped her chin in his hand and spoke to her gently, soberly, soothing away a child's nightmare. "This same I can do for you, Grisaudra. But you must serve me. We will take Chameol together. The army is nearly raised to do it. And once there, I will have need of another seer."

Dimly, she remembered what it was she had to tell Elric. But her chain-mail tunic seemed a suit of lead; like Myrrhlock's eyes it weighed her down. She could not move or speak; she drew a breath to speak and only sobbed.

"Sweet." His hand traced the line where her scar had been, once. "Come to the mirror and see how pretty you are."

As he drew Grisaudra to her feet, the crow suddenly struggled free, and in five beats of its great clumsy wings had cleared the cat's grasping claws and gained the yard.

The crow knew the tent it wanted. It landed on the snake charmer's dressing table, sending curling tongs and bottles of spirit gum flying.

"Goodness!" Hessie exclaimed. "You poor thing. Has that cat been tormenting you again?"

The bird hopped and flapped on the table, stamping in impatience, sending up clouds of talc and sequins. "Errk! Ergkg! Erkot. Errk-KOT! Ergt. Erg-GIT!"

Hessie laughed and shook her head. "All right! Heavens, what has that animal been doing to you? Yes, yes, erkit-erkit to you, too." Hessie's eyes suddenly grew thoughtful, and she recalled something from the days before she had lulled snakes with laudanum, when she had welcomed babies with lullabies and wiped the sweat from their mothers' brows. Even as Hessie didn't like to use tricks with her snakes, she had not liked to dose women in their childbed. But from time to time there had come a case of particular difficulty, and she had reluctantly reached for a certain, singular remedy.

"What—oh! Oh, it can't be! Crows can't—but if you are—and you mean—then—"

The snake charmer sat down in the chair, petting the agitated bird to calm it. Her mind spun with thoughts too wild to entertain but too dire to cast aside. Could it really be that the whole troupe had been under some enchantment, to make them forget Toby and accept a stranger unquestioningly? Could Hodge and Pyle have stumbled on the truth and so met their deaths? It was madness, wild imagination, nothing more. But if it wasn't . . .

Whom could she tell? Perhaps someone who had never known Toby—the bearded woman and the young daredevil rider. They both had something about them—a watchfulness, a keenness of the eye—that said they were more than they seemed, that they might be trusted. Yes, she would tell them.

Hessie scooped up the bird and coaxed it into one of the wicker hampers she used for carrying the adders.

"Now, not a peep out of you until I say so, and then you

had better repeat your little performance, or I shall look a jolly fool."

Elric and the Badger stared first at Hessie and then at the crow. The one stood with her hands on her hips, blushing, while the other perched on the table, hunched and ruffled and muttering low to itself.

Hessie sighed. "Come *on* dearie, before they have me carted off to the loony bin!"

The crow growled, spinning out the sound oddly. "Errrrrr—"

"That's it! Now, tell them just what you told me."

The feathers went down a little, and the crow began to mutter faster. "Errrrrrr. Git, git, git. Erkot. Er-KOT. Ergt. Errrrrrrr-git. Er-GIT."

"There!" Hessie looked from the Badger to Elric and back again. "Did you hear that?"

Elric grinned helplessly. "Clear as a bell. Errrrr. Git, git, git. Erkot, Ergt, Ergit. An irregular verb if ever I heard one. Must have been a schoolmaster's pet." He reached over to nudge the Badger in the ribs, but the younger knight's face showed him uninclined to laugh. Elric watched in amazement as the Badger's face lit up like a lamp, then watched incredulous as he seized Hessie, spun her around in a giddy dance, and kissed her.

"It's erkot, erkit, ERGOT! Sweet heaven, it *is* ergot!"

Elric was wide-eyed and slack-jawed. "What on earth has gotten into you?"

"Ergot, ergot! It's the cause of the madness, Elric, don't you see? It explains the Oncemoon business; it explains my fever; it explains everything!"

But Hessie had a stitch in her side and a worry in her brain. "Stop, oh, stop, please! Badger, seriously." He let her go, and she bent double, gripping her side. "Don't you see what it means?" she panted. "Someone has killed Hodge and Pyle. Who knows who might be next?"

Elric's face was white and mirthless when he caught the Badger's gaze. "Where's Grisaudra?"

They found her tent empty.

"She's only run away," Elric said bitterly, nudging an overturned chair with the toe of his boot.

The Badger shook his head. "She's gone, but not willingly, Elric. Would she have left her chain-mail tunic, or gone without her herb belt?"

Hessie frowned. "This makes me uneasy. Let's go to the kitchen tent."

There was no sign of the cook or the cat. Where there had been not an hour before pots and crockery—or at least the illusion of them—there was now the glass jumble of an alchemist's chamber. What bread there was had staled to bricks, the milk had turned to cheese in the pail; it seemed most of the food to leave that kitchen had been soup from stones and chops conjured from sawdust and cardboard, with enough meal mixed in to keep body and soul together, and charmed so the troupe would not feel their hunger too much.

Elric had put out a hand to pick up an alembic full of a purplish distillation when Hessie stopped him with a harsh word.

"Careful how you handle that—ergot can be given through the skin as well as on the tongue."

Elric drew back his hand. "What is this ergot, then, and how do you know so much about it?"

"It's a powerful drug, distilled from diseased rye. In its mildest form it's used to dose women in labor; I was a midwife once, and that was how I first came to know it. But after I gave up midwifery and before I took up snakes, I worked for a time for an undertaker, a sometime barber and surgeon, who taught me all manner of things that lie between medicine and magic. He taught me how a pure dose, even a small one, could convulse the gut, disorder speech, summon apparitions."

Elric turned to the Badger. "And how did *you* come to know of it? Don't tell me you learned midwifery in the monkery!"

"No—but sometimes a handful of molded rye would ease a mare having a hard time of it with a breech foal." The Badger shook his head. "I wonder I didn't think of it before."

"Why should you have?" Elric said. "For that matter, *how* could you have? Perhaps that was why you got the fever— to keep you from remembering."

Hessie called to them from the corner. "Here. I may have found something."

It lay glittering in the sawdust in the corner of the tent, a hollow glass bell covered with prickles like a chestnut.

"Hollow, like a viper's tooth. That must be how the dose was given."

"Yes," said Elric, scrubbing thoughtfully at the hair at the nape of his neck. "No good to trust to such an irregular method of dosage as the supply of rye grain. No, once the accidental dose was given, it had to be administered regularly."

The Badger's look grew grimmer. "We must be off, then, before the trail is cold. Grisaudra is in great peril."

"I know," Elric said quietly, but with a hint of temper, so that the Badger raised an eyebrow and Hessie looked at him with fresh and mildly startled eyes.

The mongrel potion in his eyes had continued to dye Elric's dreams odd colors. Last night they had showed him Grisaudra struggling to free herself from the unwanted embrace of the shroud maker. She had been forced at last to use a dagger in her own defense and to hide from her pursuers among the bodies in their shrouds. Elric had lain awake afterward wondering if he might have misjudged her completely, and if so, what other secrets the conjurer of Oncemoon Marsh kept hidden behind that wall of rage and pain.

Then Hessie looked around, her brow knit with worry. "What can it mean? The crow is gone."

Poppies. They were the last thing Grisaudra saw before she felt a sudden, sharp pricking behind her ear, before the darkness engulfed her and she felt herself lifted on a great rush of air.

She seemed to be flying, borne at a great height over a field of rye, where row on row of dark-robed figures were scything the grain, their arms swinging the curved blades in unison. The second field was charred and blackened, the smoke and steam still hissing from the ruins as if the wind of flame had just raced over it. The ground grew nearer as she was borne over the third field, close enough for her to make out the litter of bodies, looters moving among the fallen, erratic but purposeful as ants.

At last she began to descend. Below her there took shape an isolated group of dark buildings within a high wall. A convent, a prison, a castle? Grisaudra sank nearer and saw it was none of these, for she had come close enough to see the banner that flew from the bell tower: a hand and a stone. These were not nuns or prisoners or princes. This was a house of lepers.

She floated down so softly that Grisaudra wondered for the first time whether she had died and this was the next world. It had so far looked exactly like the only other world Grisaudra had known, but all her life had been a string of cruel jokes, and this might prove to be just another such.

She found herself beneath the vaulted roof of a great hall without any memory of how she had arrived there. The weight on her shoulders proved to be a heavy dark cloak lined with silk in a pattern of poppies; despite its heavy folds, she felt chilled to the marrow. In a mirror framed by tapers, Grisaudra caught sight of herself: unmarred, flushed with the ripe bloom of youth, the candles' glow turning her ash-pale hair bright and insubstantial as moonlight.

"You see, Grisaudra, that I keep my promises."

Myrrhlock stood before her, and behind him stood rank on rank of silent figures in lepers' robes, with blue glass globes around their necks like lepers' bells.

The Necromancer's magic had conjured the very picture of the Badger, down to the smallest points: a tiny scar above one eye from a distant childhood accident; the nick in his ear left by an overaffectionate mare. But the eyes were not the Badger's eyes. Myrrhlock could copy their meadow-sky blue but not the clear, laughing light that came from them. Grisaudra shuddered, remembering how the old hermit of Oncemoon Marsh had met his end, a shape-changing spell got half-right. Finding him, she had run out into the mist, too frightened to venture back for days. By then, there had been nothing left of him.

Now the figure before her wavered and went transparent; for a breath's space she saw a double image: the false Badger and Myrrhlock both. But the Necromancer was weary; the harelip cleft his face from brow to chin, his eyes were dull and his cheeks hollow, as though his face had fallen in on itself, eaten away with evil. Even here, in this sanctuary of his own making, the Necromancer's powers were waning. Grisaudra clung to this thought as Myrrhlock took her hand and drew her through the crowd. The ranks of robed figures parted noiselessly to make way for them.

As they passed into a smaller chamber Myrrhlock gave up the Badger's form entirely and put on a cap of blue goblinstone. He seemed immediately soothed and stretched out a hand to indicate that Grisaudra should be seated. She shook her head, and the Necromancer laughed softly, though not gently.

"Ah. I understand this gesture, I think. You will not sit at my feet, you will not bow to me, you mean to show me that I am not your master. Very good! Very good—then let's see you put off that cloak."

She could not, no matter how she tugged at the clasp. Only at Myrrhlock's word—a word old out of meaning, dreadful to the ear—did the cloak of poppies fall from her shoulders to lie in a crimson wreath around her feet.

The Necromancer retrieved the cloak and folded it carefully. "Quite a treasure, this. The dreamcloak of Yolanda of Twelvemoon, the half-elf queen who was as beautiful as she was mad. I had heard tales of such a cloak but feared the moths would have gotten the best of it after all these centuries. Imagine my delight when I chanced on it. It was being worn by a beggar woman in the madhouse where I first took asylum. Here, you can see where it had to be mended after the foolish lion tamer took his shears to it. It was bad enough that he might make a patchwork of it, worse still if he should show it to someone who would recognize it for what it was. But in making a turban of it, Hodge unwittingly fashioned a dream-cap with the power to summon death itself from his own imagination.

"Now, the fire-eater, he was another matter. He was rash enough to try to barter my little secret to your friend Elric in exchange for a knighthood. So, I mixed up a leaf or two of salad, rocket dressed with—but you can guess what it was dressed with."

Grisaudra felt heavy with dread, her leaden tongue barely able to form speech. "You killed them. . . ."

Myrrhlock raised a finger, a master correcting a student. "No, their own foolishness, their own weakness did them in. The lion tamer's heart was overwound with fear; he died of fright. The fire-eater met his end at the hands of his own imagination."

"And I—how shall I meet my end?"

The goblinstone caught the firelight as the Necromancer shook his head. "You have nothing to fear from me, Grisaudra. You are too valuable to me. You see, the stable boy will follow you out of a displaced sense of heroism. He will bear a message for me to Chameol." The Necromancer laughed, showing poison-stained teeth and a purple, hanged-man's tongue. "Quite a small vial will be enough. Iiliana opens all her messages herself."

Drusian

*A*t first Caitlin thought the chamber was empty. She stood in the center and turned slowly around, taking in the gem-laden game board, the blank pages of the crystal book, and the empty throne, hewn of rock, on which there rested a single raven's feather. Off to one side there was a scrape and shuffle and a baby's muffled cry.

"Bram!" The name tore from Caitlin's throat and struck her ear strangely in the echo, as though someone else had cried it.

A high-pitched shriek of laughter split the chamber, followed by an unintelligible muttering, the sounds together the two things that formed her own most ancient memory: the chiding, wild, and unreasoned voice of her guardian and keeper. At the sound, Caitlin forgot everything, her eyes filling with tears of childhood, tears of rage.

"Abagtha! He's mine! You give him back to me! You had no right to take him, no right!"

A quieter shriek echoed off the walls of the room, so that it was impossible to tell the direction from which it had come. The chamber offered no crevice or hiding place that Caitlin could see, only shadows.

The familiar mutter began to form words in the voice she knew so well. "Hee-eee, Eee-hee-he-he-heeeeeeeeee! Hee-eee-ah-ah-ah! Childling, I have your sweet babykin, your hairless pink pup. A sweet-smelling morsel he is, and toothsome, I'd wager. Hee-eee-eee!" Now Caitlin could hear Bram's voice rising with the witch's in a wail.

Caitlin knew how to speak to the old woman's unreason. "You can't have the amulet; it's gone. But I have another trinket, Batha, something you'll like even better. A seer's glass from the ancient ones under the sea. Come see!"

As she spoke, Caitlin struggled to remember that her old guardian was long dead, that the figure before her was some illusion, but the moment she saw the familiar figure, bent and hideous but beloved all the same, Caitlin's heart leaped up. Then she saw Bram.

His sojourn in the Otherworld had taken the roses from his cheeks; he was not so plump as he had been and had lost something of his lively humor, but as soon as his sweet, solemn face fastened on Caitlin's, own he began to squirm and chortle. Caitlin drew the glass salamander from her pocket and held it out to the old woman. Her heart was beating so loudly in her ears she could hardly hear her own words.

"Give him to me. He is only a baby, a noisemaker and a bothersome crock-breaker. This is far better, a bargain. Give him to me!"

Abagtha's ancient eyes looked from the luminous ornament in Caitlin's hand to the dark crown of the small head lying in the crook of her arm. She needed only a moment to weigh her choice before she snatched the ornament, nearly dropping Bram as she made the exchange.

It vanished the moment Caitlin took the child into her arms, the dull ache that had swollen her heart since the hour of Bram's loss. With hands trembling from impatience as much as from dread, she undid the elvish swaddling cloth and looked Bram over swiftly for marks of a changeling's initiation or a claim of royal ownership. But it seemed Ylfcwen's handmaidens had done nothing more dire to him than to fit his little ears with gold-foil peaks, after court fashion. Caitlin sighed and buried her face in the plump crease where his neck met his shoulder, the smell of his sweet baby hair summoning up the moment Iiliana had first put him in her arms. Bram's happy crowing turned into a hiccough, his breathing fell into the easy cadence of slumber, and his tiny fist curled around a lock of his mother's hair.

Caitlin raised her eyes to chastise Abagtha and looked instead into a pair of dazzling, luminous eyes that were the only lively thing in a figure that seemed carved of marble. Caitlin's arms closed more tightly around Bram.

Even folded, the enormous wings reached halfway to the roof of the chamber. The raven-black feathers were stark against the marble pallor of the skin, so that the being whose wings these were might have been a fantastic beast from out of Abagtha's book of incantations—half woman, half griffin. Where there should have been talons, there were graceful, ghostly hands, and where there ought to have been a woman's eyes, there were strange, knowing, luminous orbs that turned on Caitlin a gaze neither human nor inhuman.

It was out of weariness and astonishment rather than reverence that Caitlin sank to the floor, Bram cradled in her arms.

"Drusian."

"None other."

"But they called you Master."

"There is no word in the ancient rune tongues for mistress." The wings stirred and raised a slight wind. "And if there were, it would name only half of me." Drusian's brilliant eyes fell to the glass salamander in her hands. She turned it over and over, as if seeking a secret catch that once opened would reveal an ancient treasure.

"What is it, really?" Caitlin asked.

"A seer's glass, as you thought. But it is more than that,

the touchstone of a longer-lost, more-forbidden art. It is a shape-changer's lodestone to her true shape."

"What became of Newt?"

"He had brought you to me, which was all he was made to do."

"Made? But that glass was shaped long before I was born."

"Yes, but made in the hope of your coming. Did Abagtha never teach you the meaning and power of names? Chameol is named for the chameleon, the lizard that changes its colors."

"A salamander is not a chameleon."

"No—but when she was still young her enemies laid siege to Chameol, sought out her children, and destroyed them. It was wiser for the children of Chameol to choose a different symbol by which they could know one another. What could be more natural than to choose the salamander, the creature that can survive the heart of the fire? But my tale gets ahead of itself. Listen, otherworld daughter, and I will tell you what I am—and what you are meant to be."

For some minutes the wings had been growing smaller so that now, folded tightly, they were completely hidden behind Drusian's back. As the great wings had shrunk, the pallid skin had grown rosy, taking on the likeness of flesh in the bloom of health. The eyes had lost some of their brilliance, so that when Drusian reached out to the pages of the crystal book and made some adjustments Caitlin could not see, the crystal leaves began to glow like a lamp until they lit the whole chamber. When Caitlin looked back at Drusian, the pale winged figure was gone. She faced instead a human woman clad in flowing robes in the style Caitlin knew only from books on the Elder Age. Drusian's hair was broadly streaked with silver, the cunning of her eyes softened with age to wisdom. Drusian's hand fingered the ivory seal's-head amulet around her neck, and as she did so Caitlin saw her upper arms bore the tattooed runes of a shape-changer. Caitlin felt unsettled; something in those dark, bright eyes was familiar.

"Yes." Drusian smiled. "You think you know me, and you are right."

"It was you who had the glass salamander brought to me as a seal's love-gift. . . ."

"No, the glass salamander had been lost for generations, until that same lovesick seal found it."

"But you took Bram, knowing I would follow and hoping I would bring the glass salamander."

"There is some truth in your version of things—but not *all* the truth. Have you never heard of that old shape-changer's trick, sleight-of-shape? The glass salamander has been in your pocket all this time. It was I, in Newt's form, who guided you. But that was not the only form I took. I was Pj'aurinoor and Cerulean—even Serpentine."

Caitlin's eyes held a gathering storm. "Is it too much for me to ask why?"

Drusian's smile was gentle. "I should wonder only if you didn't. What do you know of the Elder Age?"

"All Iiliana could teach me. The Elders were of the time before the Pentacle, before Myrrhlock became Necromancer."

"You have been to the Devil's Sieve and seen the carvings there."

Caitlin searched Drusian's eyes for a hint of the shape-changer's purpose. "Can you read minds, then, as well as change your shape? Or do you have spies to learn these things?"

"As it happens, neither. But I do have my crystal book." Drusian put out a hand to touch the page, and there upon the crystal leaves the Badger led a blindfolded Caitlin through the catacomb maze of the Devil's Sieve. Then the picture changed to show fantastic pictures carved on the walls of the catacombs, pictures of airy palaces in the clouds, coral mansions beneath the waves.

"There is a story to be read in those pictures, if you knew it," said Drusian. "Shall I tell it to you? You must know two things before I begin: Chameol was not always an island; even as I once had a twin, so did she, and her twin with mine perished the same day beneath the waves. Also you must know there was once only one world, and the race that became Ylfcwen's people dwelled Above, before there was an Otherworld."

Bram had awakened and was looking intently from Drusian's face to Caitlin's, as if he understood what they were saying. The question rose suddenly, disturbing and unbidden, in Caitlin's mind, how much of the Otherworld Bram would carry with him when he returned to the realm of air and light. She noticed with a start that his eyes, which had been an indeterminate color at birth, had become the same blue as his father's. To see the Badger's eyes gazing out at her from Bram's face was unsettling, and Caitlin turned her attention back to Drusian's tale.

"Long ago, Chameol was not an island, but a city within a city, where the highest of all the arts were kept and nurtured. Outside her walls unpaved pilgrim's roads descended to the wide avenues and boulevards of Iule, with its bright guildhalls and busy harbor, and the palace like a rosy pearl in the setting sun."

"Chameol and Iule together linked what you know as the near and far Moons, which were then states of a single kingdom. My father's kingdom." Shadows of emotion stirred on Drusian's features, her eyes clouding over with submerged rage, surfacing grief. "In bringing us into the world, our mother was ushered from it. I drew my first breath five minutes before my twin, and she had not breathed her first before we were made motherless.

"Our grieving father named us, giving me Drusian, after the Elder word for the weeping willow. My sister he called Nairne, the Elder word for ashes.

"From birth I was taught that I was heir to the crown of Iule, and that in time I should climb the steps to the throne and take my place there. I had long lessons at a young age, in diplomacy and governance, but all the time I was supposed to be memorizing borders and rates of exchange I was thinking of the walled city that had been my mother's home. She was one of the 'walled women,' those who had chosen a life apart from the larger world of palace and guildhall, pursuing those magic arts that were even then and ever since the province of women. But then, you can recite them as well as I."

The words fell from Caitlin's lips, familiar as a prayer, and in this moment oddly comforting. "Naming, to call something by its true name; Healing, to cultivate the saving herbs; Summoning, to call forth man and beast; Changing, to change one shape for another; and Seeing, which is not a learned art but one bestowed."

Drusian smiled. "Like you, I could recite them in my sleep, though if my father had caught me, it would have meant a tanning. For he wanted me to have nothing to do with 'the witches behind the wall,' as he called them.

"But Chameol was as irresistible to me as the first sight of my mother had been to my father. So it was that on my sixteenth birthday, instead of being feasted and heralded as the next head to wear the crown of Iule, I ate a simple supper with my father and Nairne and my old nurse, and when we had eaten I wept and left them, for the next morning I should be trothed, not to any man in the kingdom, but to Chameol, and within her walls I should live the balance of my days, perfecting the ancient arts. So, the crown of Iule would fall to Nairne.

"For the first year Nairne grieved for me and would see no one, devoting herself to her painting and her loom. A year passed from the time of my going away, and Nairne was fitful in the palace, choosing to walk by the sea where we had gathered starfish and played a mermaid game as children. Borrowing her handmaiden's plain cloak, the king's daughter could walk without attracting notice, lost amidst the bustle of the port, free to watch the ships come and go.

"Another winter and summer passed away, ushering in the third year of my apprenticeship within Chameol's walls. Nairne turned her hands to the garden, coaxing along the lilies, husbanding the roses. At last, our father went to her in the garden and pointed to the flowers, blazing in their late-summer glory. Think of the winter! he chided her, and be mindful of the frost. How can you tend the flowers with more care than you give the House of Iule? If you do not marry, Nairne, Iule will be as a garden without a gardener, lost to the birds and weeds and in the end forgotten and paved over.

"Nairne lay on the ground after he had gone and wept, and when she had dried her tears she cut every bloom and blossom from its stem and bore them to the king's room, laying them at his feet and saying, send who you will; I will see these suitors. But promise me that the choice will be mine alone.

"A procession then began of suitors seeking the hand of the king's daughter. Some wished to be king of Iule; others wished to be a husband to Nairne, for her grieving had lent her face a sweet and holy sadness that many mistook for mere beauty. But one among the suitors was unswayed by Nairne's charms; he wished to rule Iule only to ruin her— a wolf among the lambs. But to Nairne, who had never known a wolf, he alone of all the suitors was handsome, he alone knew the workings of her heart, knew them indeed better than Nairne did herself, or so she wrote me: 'When he looks into my eyes, sister, I feel him look into my very soul.' I was not alarmed, as I would have been had I seen the man and seen what he was. But I had only Nairne's foolish, love-stricken letters, which told me of nothing more serious than an infatuation my father should surely see for what it was and just as surely quash.

"It was my old nurse who alerted me to the danger, both of us risking much in meeting at Chameol's gate. I learned that Nairne's suitor had presented himself at the court as a magician, for over his speaking mirrors and tarot decks he could, in the chaperone's presence, lean close to Nairne and whisper in her ear in a manner no other suitor would dare. As a member of the royal household, he could sit across from Nairne at table and ply her with tales of romance and mystery. Gravely worried, my nurse stole away one evening to meet me, begging me to come and see matters for myself. A summoner, she called him, which is a very old name for a necromancer. I was not very worried until she uttered the word, but when she said 'summoner,' my heart was chilled as it had never been, and I knew I must see Nairne's suitor myself. I agreed to steal away that evening, dressed in beggar's rags, arranging that my nurse should meet me at a gate and hide me in the banqueting hall."

Drusian paused, and for a moment Caitlin saw in the shape-changer's human eyes a trace of that other, inhuman brilliance, and Drusian's face took on some of the pallor of her other form.

"You must understand the nature of my position within the walls of Chameol. I was a third-year apprentice, it is true, but I was also the king's daughter, and accorded nearly the same honor as was given to the Keepers of the Arts, those women who knew the secrets of the four Learned Arts and of the Art above Arts, Seeing. The Keeper of Changing was in failing health, and in the spring of that year she had called me to the bed to which she was confined and told me that I was to study with her alone that year, and upon her death I was to become a Keeper and a changer of shapes.

"Within my year of study I was to speak to no one and

speak of nothing that was of Iule and the world outside, lest I unwittingly betray Chameol. The process of becoming a Keeper was fraught with danger, for in power lay temptation, and in temptation lay the life of Chameol itself. It was on penalty of banishment—stripped of her name, her health, her power to summon, her true shape, and sometimes of sight itself—that a Keeper passed outside the walls of Chameol. I knew this penalty well, for in her youth my nurse had dwelt in Chameol, apprenticed to a Keeper, and had failed the final test. But my love of Nairne and my fear for my sister and Iule both gave me the measure of courage I lacked."

The scene she had summoned to mind was still vivid and repelling to its teller, and Drusian's expression changed to one of remembered loathing. "I found them not in the banqueting hall, but in one of the smaller dining chambers, our father absent and no chaperone but the oldest servant, a woman completely deaf and nearly blind, to wait on them. I barely knew the woman seated there as Nairne, so changed was she, dressed in robes so unseemly my father should never have allowed them. But it was her expression more than her manner of dress that was most altered. She was deep in the thrall of the man who sat close at her side, feeding her from a dish of honeyed figs.

"I entered the room with a swiftly beating heart, for despite my beggar's garb it seemed impossible that my twin should not know me. But she met my eyes with a cold gaze and such an expression of peevish ill nature and selfish vanity that it was I who did not know my own twin. Nairne had not a cruel bone in her body nor a thoughtless drop of blood; Nairne lived to please others and grieved to offend. But this was no longer the sister whose life I had shared, heartbeat for heartbeat, from the cradle. I had only to look into her eyes to see that.

"My costume fooled even Nairne; she did not recognize

me, but curtly demanded how I had gained entrance and what business I had there. 'Though I am hungry, I do not beg,' I answered her. 'Let me tell your fortune in return for the scraps you would throw to the dogs.'

"Any child of my father would instantly have offered a seat at table and would have fetched the best meat and drink the palace had to offer, for our father treated the least of his visitors as he did the greatest of them. But it flattered this new Nairne to have her fortune told. While I laid the cards out upon the damask cloth the eyes of the magician never once left me, and as I placed the cards in the four corners of the table for the four winds, I fought to keep my hands from trembling, for I knew now what kind of man this was. Every feature of his face was graven in my mind and has never been erased: the coldest eyes I ever have seen, a mouth split with cruelty. It was not to win Nairne's hand that he had come to Iule; it was not a queen or even a crown that he sought. This was the destroyer, the murderer of hope, whose coming had been foretold."

Caitlin lifted her eyes, as if suddenly recalled to memory and startled to speech. The words came to her lips of their own accord: *"To this day they say that if the spinner in the wood is ever awakened, the murder of love and life itself shall be avenged—"*

Drusian's eyes gleamed bright with tears, and she smiled down on Bram as he lay in Caitlin's arms. "*—and the world set aright.* Daughter of light and air! This is at last the night that shall dawn on a new Iule! But I neglect my tale. Listen. These words shall raise up the two things I loved best in all the world: Nairne, my sister, and Iule, my home.

"At Nairne's bidding, then, I spread out the cards and read from them the fortune that came into my head, but still the cards spoke true as any seer: sorrow by water and a long banishment. At these words the Necromancer smiled and pressed Nairne's hand as though to comfort her, but I knew his true meaning! It took all my love for my twin, all my will not to strike him and call him by what he was. But I held my tongue and told Nairne's fortune. When I had done, I was rewarded not with meat nor even with crusts but with some rancid trimmings not fit for pigs. For these I expressed my gratitude and bowed my way out of the room. In the shadows I waited until I had stopped trembling, and casting off my costume I climbed the stairs to my father's apartments. I found him alone.

"One look and I knew the worst. The summoner could not have gained such a place of favor at Nairne's side without the king's assent, so his objections somehow had been overcome, his blessing obtained by poisoning his mind.

"My father was seated at the table, a small ivory portrait of my mother before him, a casket of jewels on its side, its treasure spilling over the tabletop: our mother's wedding jewels and Nairne's dowry. A tall flask stood at hand, nearly empty, and the king greeted me with a warmth that came as much from the wine as from his heart.

"He rose unsteadily and kissed me, pleased that I had come for my sister's wedding. Argue as I might, I could not convince him that Nairne's suitor was a summoner and the sworn enemy of Iule. At one point I could see a struggle play over his features as he fought to remember, as some word of mine sparked a fleeting memory. But the wine— and whatever had been mulled with it—had done its work. The king's animated spirit, his intelligent humor, his very soul had been emptied out, and the enemy of Iule had filled him with a draught of his own concocting, so that his veins ran with a forgetfulness that had completely unbalanced his mind. The king was mad.

"I climbed the pilgrim's path to Chameol in the dead of night, beneath a watchful, foreboding moon. I slipped through the gates and into my bed undetected—at least undetected by any mortal gaze. But the summoner watched me, in some form he found it handy to assume. Perhaps it was the marble statue in the garden, whose eyes seemed to gleam at me as I passed. But I think it was a raven's shape he took.

"That night I lay awake, pondering how to free my sister and my homeland from the evil influence that had fallen over them. At last I lit a lamp and stole away to the library that held the five Books of the Keepers, which none but a Keeper could touch. If an uninitiated hand touched one of the tomes, the silver clasps would burn, and if an untutored eye fell on the pages within, the runes themselves would begin to shriek and howl, for the spells kept therein were some of them deadly, and the arts of Summoning and Changing not to be taken lightly. But I had been well taught and knew to dust my hands and the books with powder of bookworm and was thus able to consult the books without raising an alarm. I found the spell I needed, though I shuddered to read it, and only when I had memorized it did I douse my light and steal back to my own chamber.

"The day dawned that was to see Nairne married to the summoner. My sister woke with an unaccountable urge to walk by the sea. Her bridegroom grew suspicious and listened intently at her window to discern whether she were being summoned, but he could hear nothing, for it was I who summoned her with her own soul's name, which no ear but her own could hear and which she could no wise resist. When she had made her way down to the sea, she walked straight into the waves, and though her handmaidens wept and cried out to her, she heeded nothing but my summons. Out Nairne walked into the embrace of the waves, and thus Nairne appeared to vanish.

"The frightened handmaidens ran back to the palace and related what they had seen. The bridegroom came with them to the shore, where they found Nairne nearly drowned on the beach.

"Or so they thought, for it was I, needing only a small changing spell to become my twin, after all. And what of Nairne? She had been given the shape of a seal and was safely hidden in the sea-flax beds until all danger was past and I could come for her.

"They revived me and brought me back to my father's house, and for two days the wedding was put off. On the third day I could feign illness no longer, and the marriage was performed. There was some part of the king that was not mad, that had not been conquered, and on hearing the oaths exchanged, this part of him ceased to struggle with his mad, enslaved soul. So my wedding night was spent in a vigil at the king's bedside, and by morning's light my shoulders were heavy with the weight of grief and my brow bowed beneath the crown of Iule.

"When my father had been laid to rest, I begged my husband that I should walk in the garden alone with my thoughts, and he agreed. I worried that in my grief my mind should grow distracted and the spell's thread break. Nairne's fate and Iule's depended on my firmity of mind. So I strolled in the garden and paused to sit by the statue in the garden, a likeness of my mother in marble planted around with everlasting and laurel and rosemary. For a dark hour my courage failed me, and I wept. I did not see the raven come to light on the shoulder of the statue.

"Grief made me careless, and when I heard my name called in Nairne's sweet voice I looked up, straight into the Summoner's eyes, an answer on my lips. And it was that answer that imprisoned me, for when I reached back with my hand to steady myself, and touched the marble, I became it, statue and raven both, as you saw me. And Nairne, with no one to free her or guess her fate, was likewise doomed.

"Myrrhlock—for that was the summoner's name—had one last task ahead of him: the destruction of Iule itself. From the depths of the earth he summoned forth fire and tremors, and in an hour the city itself had sunk beneath the waves. Chameol he could not destroy, for her magic was a match for him. He had in mind for Chameol another fate. Iule should be forgotten utterly, the very name erased without a trace. Chameol should live in legend only, an island kingdom whose very existence should be ever disbelieved. And so the house and name of Iule were forgotten even by Chameol herself, and the Arts abandoned.

"Without the just hand of Iule to guide them, the surrounding lands were broken up into the Thirteen Moons, and the age of the Pentacle dawned. It was a dark time for Chameol. The Keepers fled, taking the four of the five Books with them. One by one, the Keepers themselves and the Books they guarded succumbed to time and forgetfulness and the tooth of the worm. The books' remaining pages were scattered, cut into fragments that were sold as relics or for spells. Some of the pages survived and were bound together with remnants from other volumes into a book that passed from thief to trader and was so lost, its own magic reduced to a remedy for toothache. Keepers! Better you should be dust than live to see your books so, bound in pigskin and iron."

A look of amazement spread over Caitlin's features. "Abagtha's book . . . the book of incantations . . ."

"Just so."

"But you said there were five Books. What happened to the fifth?"

Drusian pointed to the crystal book, whose pages glowed with a steady light. "It was the Book of Seeing. Ylfcwen's people knew its value and brought it here for safekeeping."

"So that was why you summoned me, to fetch the last Book of the Keepers. . . ."

"Only partly. When Iule sank beneath the waves, a great chasm split the kingdom, creating a world underground. Eventually the magic banished from the one world found a place in the other. Ylfcwen and her kind are beyond the dominion either of good or evil, but when Iule fell and Chameol was sunk in mist they deemed the gemfields a better home for their kind than the world of men. I fled with them to bide my time until the day should come for my and Iule's release. Century on century I have sat in this dark chamber, ruling the Otherworld but a prisoner of it, a tribute of gems laid at my feet when all I desired was my freedom."

"And I was summoned to release you."

"No—there was no need to Summon you. It was enough to take Bram. Love alone brought you here. If you had harbored any other motive, you would never have found me. For love's sake Iule was lost. Love alone can raise her. But it must be done willingly, and you must know what it will cost you."

Drusian reached out to touch the crystal book. The leaves came to life with the scene of an ancient palace, the marble walls hung with tapestries of sea-flax and carpeted with scarlet coral. Schools of golden fish slanted in the windows and across the rooms like shafts of sunlight.

"This is my father's house, which lies now beneath the waters of the strait of Chameol. Fetch me the crown of Iule: once it is raised from the sea, Myrrhlock will be destroyed and I shall be freed from my prison in the Otherworld. I am too old to take my true form Above, but once free of Myrrhlock's spell I can change my form for all time. It is my wish to join Nairne and her kind."

Caitlin pondered the shape-changer's words in silence, her eyes rapt on the shifting image of the watery palace. One of the toppled statues had lost an arm, and the figure, a woman, gazed sorrowfully down on an exquisite marble of a child. The laughing boy reached out over his mother's disembodied arm, his fingers outstretched to grasp the tails of passing fish. Caitlin tore her eyes away, as if wrestling with a powerful charm. "If I do this," she said slowly, "am I free to return with my son to Chameol?"

"Yes, but there is a risk—" Drusian was suddenly alert to a more present danger. Bram had reached a hand out to touch the tempting pictures that swirled on the crystal pages. Drusian siezed him by his plump wrist and drew his hand away as if from a hot stove. "Ah, ah! Careful he doesn't touch the pages, or he'll be in Iule before you."

"That will never do," Caitlin said, kissing Bram on his furrowed brow. "No—don't cry. Here—Drusian will let you borrow her throne, and here's a feather for you to play with. Don't be a goblin."

Her back was barely turned before Bram had found a better toy. The jeweled game board was too great a temptation, and it was just within his reach. His chubby hand reached for an ebony pawn, but he only knocked it over. It rolled from the golden circle across the game board, through squares inlaid with serpentine and sapphire and tiger's eye, finally coming to rest in one of the numbered squares set with silver that formed the border of the game board.

Drusian passed a hand over the pages of the crystal book, and the vision of Iule vanished, replaced by a blue as still as the surface of a pond.

"When you have the crown, call for me and I will be summoned. You will find Bram in the place from which he was first taken. When you are ready—"

"—I am ready."

"Touch the pages of the book."

Caitlin obeyed. The calm reflection of the crystal pages broke at her touch into ripples. In the next second Caitlin felt herself plummet into space, then into water.

The pages of the crystal book went dark, and the chamber rang with a clear tone, a note struck on a tuning fork. Only then did Drusian see the mischief Bram had worked on the game board. The shape-changer gazed with horror at the

ebony piece where it had come to rest in a silver square
engraved with Ylfcwen's seal and the number seven.

"Seven years! Child, child, what have you wrought! What
a grief you've brought on your mother now!"

The Cloak
and the Crown

"It's the only way."

Elric wheeled on the Badger, his face taut with fear. "How can you know that? It's poison—it could kill us or, if it spares our bodies, kill our souls and minds and anything else that makes us human—makes us other than what *he* is."

Between them on the rough trestle table, in a silver-and-crystal cordial glass, lay a few thimblesful of purple liquor. But more lay between them than that: There was an understanding that somehow they had changed places, that the Badger had emerged from his fever and the clutches of the river bright as a finely honed sword, tempered in the fire and cooled in the water to a shining keenness. Elric's face was graven with care, and his quarrel with Grisaudra had sorely shaken his belief in himself, as a man and as a knight.

The Badger shook his head stubbornly. "You may be right, but it is the only hope we have to find Myrrhlock—and save Grisaudra."

Hessie spoke from the shadows. "I'm afraid he's right, Elric. Whatever else that swallow may do, it will certainly take you to Myrrhlock and Grisaudra." The snake charmer stepped forward, unclasping what looked like a jeweled necklace. The string of bright green gems lay brightly in her palm, then lifted its head to regard them through eyes of jet.

"The apothecary asp . . ." Elric murmured.

"You know it? Then you also know its bite cures all other poisons. It can lead the hopeless back from the brink of death itself. Except for one: To anyone who lives on poison itself, on evil and hatred—to him this bite is the only death."

Elric's grey eyes narrowed. "Come, Hessie—you were once more than a midwife. How, where, did you learn these things?"

Hessie laughed. "Sometime, perhaps, I shall tell you. But it is a long tale that will take no shortening, and now the lack we feel so keenly is time." She fastened the asp around Elric's wrist, where the reptile resumed its uncanny resemblance to a precious coil paved with green gems. Then Hessie kissed them each solemnly, Elric upon the cheek and the Badger upon his brow, as a mother kisses her soldier sons before they go off to battle. And so the charmer of snakes and other things of the shadows left them, and on her going the tent fell into a profound darkness, though outside it was broadest day. The lamp, its wick burned low, struggled to hold the shadows back from a feeble circle of light.

Within the circle Elric and the Badger sat silent and immobile until the Badger reached out and picked up the small silver-and-crystal glass, raising it to his lips and letting a few beads of the strange liquor pass over his tongue. Then he handed the glass to Elric, who did the same, and so they passed the glass back and forth until the deadly cordial was gone, each man riveting his gaze on the other, watching for some sign that the potion had worked its way into their veins.

"Nothing," said Elric at last, when some half an hour had passed with no observable change in either man's face or in the objects in the tent around them. "It must need a spell to set it off. Or else this batch has lost its potency."

"No, it is still quite potent," the Badger said calmly. He

had gone very white and sweat had begun to bead his brow. "Turn around—softly, now!"

Behind them, casting an eerie glow in the dimness of the tent, stood a watery apparition dragging a tangled burden of waterweeds, rotting barge ropes, and torn fishing nets. Ghostly water streamed over the floor of the tent, giving up a wet-rot smell of river, but wetting nothing.

"Pyle!" Elric said.

"Or what our imaginations—or this potion—have raised of him," the Badger murmured.

It was the fire-eater, somewhat the worse for his time in the river: a fishhook snagged one ear, and his left foot was hopelessly snared in an eel trap. The ghost gazed mournfully from Elric to the Badger, as if struggling to regain the speech that the river had taken away. Already the apparition grew paler, and both Pyle and the train of weeds and rope behind him began to rise slowly to the middle of the room, as though borne upward by a rising tide.

And he was gone, leaving nothing behind but a pronounced smell of river and a fainter note of kerosene.

When Pyle's ghost had gone, the Badger sat with his lips pressed tightly together, his boot heels knocking on the rungs of his chair, reliving in his mind the struggle with the current that had nearly taken his life. Then he felt Elric's hands on his shoulders, shaking him.

"No! I'm all right—I was thinking of Hodge, of that face when I saw it last."

But it was the lion and not his tamer who next appeared, his massive paws treading the air a foot above the tent floor. As Rollo wagged his head from side to side, the beams of his eyes gleamed forth like chinks of light from a watchman's lantern. This was not the rheumatic, toothless lion who had allowed a child to braid wildflowers into his mane. This was the man-eater that Rollo had never been in life, and he paced closer to the two knights with a furious fire burning in his eyes.

But already the spectral lion had begun to dissolve. Indeed, the lion's haunches had faded to near transparency, and his forelimbs rolled away into mist; the paws themselves had disappeared completely.

The rest of the apparition went out like a match, with a lingering smell of singed fur.

Something very strange had happened to the tent. The rushes strewn on the floor stood on end, green again and alive with the peeping of frogs and crickets. The tent poles had grown bark, the onions hanging from them turned to moss and the hams to roosting owls. Elric and the Badger strained to see the other side of the tent and the sunlight and air they knew must be there, but they could see nothing. They were no longer in the kitchen tent. The chairs in which they had lately sat were gone; the two knights found themselves on a small island in the middle of the Oncemoon Marsh.

A figure approached them through the mist, a will-o'-the-wisp in human form, the long white neck garlanded with swanthistle, knees ghostly behind a skirt of whispering rushflower.

Their imaginations, aided by the ergot cordial, had called forth Tillie as she never was. It was not a vacant, drowned stare that caught their wary eyes but an owl's, flashing like silver disks in the moonlight. In her hands she was weaving a rope of frog grass, the sharp blades cutting her fingers.

She was sighted like an owl but mute as a swan. With her roughened fingertips she reached out to touch the Badger's cheek; the sensation, light as a cobweb, made him shiver. He reached up to grasp that hand, but his fingers closed on air.

The eerie light in her eyes dimmed, and for a moment that owllike gaze seemed human. She turned to Elric as if in appeal, and all of a sudden it was Grisaudra who stood there, a rope of borage belted around her tunic of chain mail.

Grisaudra seized his hand tightly in her own and looked intently into his eyes. "Courage," she whispered, and pressed her lips to the palm of his hand. And was gone.

The Badger stared for a moment before he found his voice. "Are you all right?"

Elric could not answer, could only look at his hand, which bore a clear impression of chain mail and a strange silvery blister, something his mother used to call an elf kiss.

The mist had lifted and revealed them not in Oncemoon Marsh, but in the chill flagstone hallway of some long-abandoned fortress. High up in the stone walls were windows of leaded glass in the pattern of a pentacle. But despite the windows and the austere silence, this was no temple, nor was it a castle, unless it was a temple to loneliness or a castle for ghosts. Not a breath of air stirred, and it was cold, cold as the grave.

Elric was the first to place the smell, the acrid vapor from pitch pots, the smoke thought to prevent the spread of contagion. Lepers' robes of grey wool lay piled in an open chest, in readiness for new inmates, and from hooks on the wall hung lepers' bells.

"It *seems* real enough," the Badger murmured. The draft under the door was cold, likewise the torch threw forth heat and light. "I can feel the wool and smell the pitch. I am either very sane or very, very mad."

Elric shook his head. "We are somewhere other than the tent. How far we have wandered—how long we have been gone—there is no way of knowing. But if everything else is an illusion, the danger, at any rate, is real."

"Oh, it is real indeed!"

Myrrhlock stood before them, the hood of the silk-and-velvet cloak pushed back to reveal a skullcap of goblinstone. His hands rested on the shoulders of a slight figure neither Elric nor the Badger could at first recognize. The cloak of poppies fell forward from the Necromancer's shoulders and enveloped her as though it were the embodiment of the spell that held her.

Grisaudra was clothed in an unearthly beauty, a changeable aura that shone from her in hues of moonsilver and alabaster, so that her hair and skin and robes seemed to be made of the same changeable and precious matter. All that was left of the Grisaudra they had known were her eyes, and these regarded them blankly, betraying nothing. Behind her, in endless rows, pressed an army of grey-robed figures, hoods obscuring their faces so it was impossible to tell what sort of beings these were, innocent captives or unspeakable creatures called forth from regions unnamed.

The smooth, cool scales of the apothecary asp seemed to burn Elric's skin. Surely it would burn through his sleeve. Myrrhlock would see it, and they would be lost. But the Necromancer's gaze never strayed from the Badger's face, his eyes bright with a cold, malevolent light.

"I have looked forward to this meeting, tanner's son. This time I think you shall find me better armed."

The world was all blue-green. She was afloat in the waves, twined fast in the billows of sea-flax, unable to tell whether her form was seal or human or to distinguish sea from sky. Caitlin fastened her gaze on two fishermen's floats, and the world steadied. Then the floats grew nearer and became two whiskered faces she knew well. Nairne's guards swam up to her, barking a greeting. Their sharp but gentle teeth cut the bonds of sea-flax. As soon as Caitlin was free, the seals turned and dove, leading the way down into Nairne's kingdom, ribbons of silver bubbles streaming in their wake. With a strong kick from the waist, Caitlin plummeted after them.

Down they went through the perpetual, blue-green twilight. Caitlin's first sight of Iule was a graveyard of ships speared on the uppermost spires of the city like so many paper pinwheels, their wrecks turning slowly this way and that in the current. They sank silently past silent belltowers and the ghostly domes of Iule's guildhalls. In the dim green light Caitlin glimpsed wonderful things—a sunken garden overgrown with sea flowers of dazzling hues: seal peonies and eel lilies. This was the garden where Nairne had once tended her roses. But there was not time enough to pause, not breath enough for anything but her one task.

Caitlin's seal escort led her through the maze of sunken buildings, through corridors whose tapestries had rotted away only to be replaced by a bright, living cloth of mosses and lacy sea fans. Through a carpet of scarlet coral Caitlin glimpsed bright mosaics: a tiger rampant, the figure of a wizard in blue robes, and a figure that might have been a mermaid or some other siren—half-woman, half-serpent.

She knew the chamber when she found it by the marble child, broken from the statue of its mother. Why had the sight so disturbed her before, when she had seen it outlined upon the crystal pages of Drusian's book? There was nothing here to worry or perturb her. Her sight dimmed and her lungs burned, and the gentle water lulled her, telling her to heed the loving call of the legion of the drowned. *Breathe me*, said the sea, *a place has been kept for you here in my coral chambers.*

"Seal's song" was the sailors' name for it, the light-headedness that makes the drowning one cease to struggle. But it was the seals who saved her, rousing her from forgetfulness with nips, reviving her with bubbles of air trapped in their thick pelts. Clinging to the neck of one seal, Caitlin spied the crown of Iule.

It was bent and corroded, so crusted with coral that the carvings were nearly undecipherable. But Drusian's crystal book had shown Caitlin the crown as it had lain on the brows of the monarchs of Iule: the golden band of mulberry leaves, signifying wisdom, and above them panels representing each of the five arts of the Keepers.

Caitlin seized the crown, her lungs burning for air, but she had no strength to kick, and the sea took up its chant with the pounding blood in her ears. Nairne's guards pressed in close, gently bearing her form between them, up through the spires of that green and silent kingdom to the realm of light and air.

"It was very simple, once I had conceived it. After all, who would suspect the bread?"

Elric and the Badger had been brought to chambers high in the tower of the leper house. These were Myrrhlock's own rooms; the ergot was distilled elsewhere, but a small table held a number of decanters, alembics, and vials of the distilled poisons on which the Necromancer fed. There was no bed; to such a creature as Myrrhlock, repose came in some form other than sleep. A fire burned on the hearth, but for utility rather than warmth. The only human comfort in the room was the chair in which Grisaudra now sat, impassive and serene, a crow perched on the chair back by her ear, a cat dozing in her lap.

Myrrhlock went to the table and busied himself with a dropper and vial.

"You put most of the pieces of the puzzle together very well. I congratulate you on that, and as a token of my esteem I will fit together the rest for you.

"Something such as I am cannot easily be destroyed. From Ninthstile I made my way to this place, where I could disguise myself without attracting notice. I happened on the ergot by accident. It is a blight that occurs in nature, and it happened that the local grain merchant unloaded his diseased rye on the leper house, thinking it the least exacting of his customers. There broke out among the inmates at this place an epidemic, which many did not survive. The connection between the disease and the grain was made by no one else; they attributed the symptoms to their leprosy and the madness to despair. Those who were spared fled in terror.

"For my part, I had chanced on the tool of my revenge. All that winter in the solitude of this place I tended my seedling rye, and in the spring I set out, selling the tainted grain to farmers, and where necessary burning crops and granaries in order to create a demand for my wares. And once the dose was given, it was simple enough to call them. They were like pigeons coming home to roost. And so I gained two things: I gathered to me a silent army against the time I should have need of them, an army of a kind that should never be suspected. And I had created the very kind of disturbance I knew should bring one or two of Iiliana's best knights." The Necromancer's harelip curled into a smile. "And here you are."

Elric's gaze was fastened on Grisaudra as he tried to read her eyes. Had she sold her soul? It seemed to him they held something of the old Grisaudra, if nothing more than her thinly veiled loathing of him. Their eyes locked for a brief moment in some recognition before she bowed her head, her attention all for her cat. Why should I have expected anything else, Elric thought, too weary to be bitter. And I, what would I do, if someone offered me everlasting beauty, even everlasting youth? With her lot in life, why should she believe in some abstract good of mine? He has won, and we have lost.

"So you will kill us," he said aloud.

"No, only you. The stableboy will carry a message for me to Chameol, after which Grisaudra may do with him what she will."

Grisaudra's eyes were fixed on the smooth plait of Caitlin's hair that cinched the Badger's wrist. Then she raised her eyes to his and a faint current of understanding passed between them.

Grisaudra stood, and the aura wavered like a flame.

"No."

The word seemed to cut her; she winced with pain, and the illusion of beauty faltered, showing a glimpse of the old Grisaudra. Myrrhlock turned on her, uttering a bitter word in a rune tongue. She fell to the ground as if under the force of a blow.

"It is not for you any longer, Grisaudra, to say no or yes to anything. The yes you gave when you swore to serve me was the last that was yours to give or withhold."

The face Grisaudra raised from the floor once more bore a scar across it. "No."

The Necromancer's wrath was turned as much inward on his own mismeasure as it was turned outward on Grisaudra's defiance. Myrrhlock spoke another rune word, and Grisaudra crumpled under the force of it, the aura writhing around her like a sheet of flame. The beauty her soul had purchased melted away like mist, leaving her as she had been the day Elric had first brought the Badger to her for a love cure.

At the window, a pigeon landed on the sill in a ruffle of wind, folding over her back wings that caught the light with the green and gold of mother-of-pearl. Myrrhlock whirled toward the sound, and in the second his back was turned Elric lunged forward, the apothecary asp in his hand like a small jeweled dagger.

Swinging back to face this newer threat, Myrrhlock upset the table and its array of deadly liquors. Elric's feet went out from under him, and a torrent of poison and shattered glass rained onto his head. The Badger sprang forward and with Grisaudra's aid pulled Elric unconscious from the debris. The bite meant for Myrrhlock spared Elric instead, but the asp had spent its own life in the saving sting.

Suddenly the room was ablaze with light, a brilliance borne on a rush of wind, wings threshing light from the very air. And there was in the room a presence, something more terrible than an angel and too beautiful to behold. The face was a woman's face, full of a holy wrath and sorrow, the smooth brow banded with a crown of leaves wrought in gold.

"Yes, I am Drusian released! I am your doom, Myrrhlock, come for you."

Myrrhlock's features were rigid with terror, and he groped behind him blindly for the cloak of poppies, as if it could shield him from that awful gaze. But his hand closed only on the back of the claw-foot chair.

The winged creature spoke three names as softly as a prayer. "For Myhrra, then, and for Tỳbitha, and for my beloved Nairne, I summon and bind you for all time."

It was the spell Myrrhlock had used in the royal garden, ages past, to bind Drusian. He instantly became the thing his hand had closed on. The Badger stared, hardly able to grasp the transformation before him. Drusian had summoned a demon of wood, the expression frozen in a howl of defeat as though a craftsman's painstaking had carved it there. It was like the Necromancer in every respect but the hands: They were changed to lion's paws, each clutching in its talons a wooden sphere. Already the wood was riddled with wormholes, and before his eyes the Badger watched Myrrhlock fall to dust. Then an acrid smoke rose up from the floor, and a sour smell of acid, and even the dust was gone.

The wind rose again and the blinding light, and then the crown clattered to the floor, and the only sound was that of the pigeon beating its way homeward to Nairne's kingdom.

When at last they could tear their eyes from the window, Grisaudra and the Badger were startled to see, huddled on the hearth in each other's arms, two girls, where there had a moment before been a crow and a cat. Grisaudra came to herself first, and going up to them took each by the hand and led them from that place.

The Badger first retrieved the crown, wrapping it in the cloak of poppies; the one thing he meant to save and the other see destroyed. Then he lifted Elric on his back and followed.

Homecoming

Slumped at his counting table, Folderol held his head in his hands and groaned. Hessie and the Badger stood before him and traded a glance.

"You can't blame me," Hessie chided gently. "How can you expect me to pass up an offer to head my own troupe? I have myself to think of, you know, and my old age to provide for. And if a few of the troupe choose to follow me, well, that's their right, now, isn't it?"

Folderol only groaned. "Gone. All of it! Gone, gone. Oh, whoahoah-iz-meeee . . ."

Hessie's patient voice took on an edge. "Here now," she said tartly, "aren't you taking this all a little hard? After all, you haven't lost everyone. You'll still have all the troupe you had a few weeks ago, save me."

Folderol raised his head and glowered balefully at her. "It's the gold!" he barked. "They took it—took it all, every cent I owned."

"Who took it?"

"That damn-cur wolf-girl and that wretched albino pup of hers. Blast them! Blast and damn 'em!" Folderol thumped the table with his fist, making the calico tufts he had torn from his beard leap on the felt tabletop like trained dogs. "I'd hidden it, but that little white rat nosed it out. It's gone, and now they're gone, and the rest of the filthy pack with them." He lowered his head again and moaned. He raised a hand and waved them away. "Go, go, all of you. Take the whole troupe. I can't pay them; they'll all leave anyhow."

Ulfra and Nix had left early that morning, with the pack of wolves and a bootful of gold, and in a few days had made their way to the edge of the great forest known as the Weirdwood. The pledge that bound the wolves to Ulfra's service had expired, and under the terms of their oath the pack was returning to their first wild home. Poor Nix hung on the neck of the she-wolf until Ulfra dragged him off. Some of the younger wolves, ones who had spent most of their short lives in the wolf-girl's service, stood around silently, ears flattened against their heads and heads sunk between their shoulders as if uncertain what trick Ulfra wanted of them. Their elders had only to catch the nutmeggy smell of the rain-damp loam before they struck out for the cover of the ancient and knowing trees. The eldest wolf turned and called to the stragglers, who hurried after. They were soon lost in the thicket of shadows. Nix's whimper broke into an unhappy wail. Ulfra cuffed him, but not too roughly, and he fell in at her side as they turned and retraced their way to the town.

Near the outskirts they began to pass some farmhouses. Each time they passed a long, low building of peat and thatch Ulfra would lift her head and sniff deeply. Nix's spirits lifted, and he smacked his lips, thinking Ulfra meant to steal a pig for them to roast. The third time she sniffed, Ulfra smelled the something she was looking for. She pinned a coin purse to Nix's shirtfront and began to chase him with businesslike cuffs and snarls toward the house.

At first Nix raced and laughed, thinking it a game, but the wallop that landed on his left ear convinced him otherwise. The boy began to whimper and then to cry. Ulfra was unrelenting. Lights appeared in the unglazed windows of the farmhouse; then the door opened and let a heavy slab of yellow light out into the dark yard.

The wolf-girl's gaze locked with the boy's, and the unyielding blue fire he saw there told him he was beaten. Nix swallowed his whimper and without a backward glance walked toward the dark figure framed in the blazing light of the farmhouse doorway.

As the closing door narrowed the light to slivers and chinks around the doorjamb and hinges, Ulfra's shoulders slumped. She stood in the thick shadows of the yard, resisting the call of the wolves that rode the highest pitch of the wind. At last Ulfra set out on the road again, walking away from the last fields and hedgerows to the town, with its smell of soot and wash water on cobblestones and the sweat of horses and men.

"Is it that fox after the hens again, Tom?" the farmer's wife called to her husband.

"No," the householder said, shaking his head. "The damndest thing. Come see."

The farmer stood and looked from the snowy hair of the boy before him to the six gold coins gleaming in his hand. Without a word he handed the note to his wife.

It was written on the back of a bill advertising a band of traveling acrobats. *Take Wondrous and Amazing Care of NIX, The Albino Deaf Mute!* it said in unsteady printing.

The couple stood a moment in silent contemplation of all this. The howl of their seventh and youngest child brought the woman to her senses first, and she took Nix by the hand.

"Come on, then," she said with a sigh, "and see how you like my wondrous and amazing soup."

Ylfcwen groaned, stretching her feet toward Emma's fire, her stomach heavy with the meat and drink that humans favor: lamb stewed with onions and rosemary; chunks of dark, seedy bread; golden ale tasting of apples and summer. "No wonder mortals don't fly. Even if they had the wings for it, with food like this they could never leave the ground." "Mmm," was all Emma said in agreement. She had lived a long time among mortal men and women and found her visitor from the Otherworld an unsettling, almost embarrassing, reminder of the past. Her own days at the elvish court seemed impossibly distant. Among her neighbors Emma was well-liked but not entirely respectable, running as she did a rooming house renowned as much for the bed boarders got as for the board. Unknown to her neighbors, Emma's boarders were all knights of Chameol, thankful for a place to let down their guises for an evening of good company.

"Be careful," she said to her guest, "not to eat too much of it, if your design is to return Below. It will make you heavy and dull and give you human cares. I am used to these things and now prefer them, but they might not agree with your constitution as well as they do mine. If you plan on returning to court, you had best not delay."

Ylfcwen sighed. "It was not my intention to go back without a human child as compensation for the goblin I lost. But it's proved to be much more difficult than I imagined. I had never realized what contrary creatures these mortals are."

"Yes." Emma smiled at some memory of her own. "That they are."

The stew had settled a little, and now that she was less painfully full of dinner, Ylfcwen began to grow drowsy and content. Ale had its charms, though it was not rootwine. Yes, she thought, it's time I returned to the Otherworld. There will be other chances to find a new favorite and choose a consort. Ylfcwen missed her mole and did not trust her prized orchids to hands other than her own.

Emma was thinking how much better she liked ale than rootwine and how she preferred her companions wild from the field and not forced in the hothouse. Over the rim of her glass the elder of the two elf queens looked at her successor and thought she wouldn't have changed places with her for all the world.

Caitlin was in bed. A humming slowly formed into low voices, then into the mutter and chirp of birds. As Caitlin moved her head, light and shadow dappled her closed eyes. She opened them and met Iiliana's worried gaze.

"Thank heaven!" Iiliana said, giving her a white-lipped kiss that was warm, for all that. "What a scare you gave us!"

"I nearly fainted when I found you, lying there so still, with half the bottle of the ergot gone. I couldn't forgive myself, leaving it within your reach like that, when you were distraught out of your mind."

Iiliana was braiding Caitlin's hair. They were seated in the window, and Caitlin was gazing down into the garden as if into the bottom of the sea, as if the birds on the lawn were strange fish moving among the languid fronds. She spoke, but slowly, the way she had when she had first returned to Chameol from her sojourn among the seals, before she lost her seal speech.

"Distraught?"

"About your son," Iiliana said gently.

"Bram."

Iiliana looked startled. "Oh, no! He's quite fine. It was the other, the twin—"

"Twin," Caitlin repeated dully.

Iiliana took Caitlin's hand and squeezed it. "Yes. You remember. They were twin boys, only one did not live long. You named the other one Bram. His wet nurse is bringing him in to see you. He's missed his mother."

The baby they put in her arms was Grimald. Not quite the Grimald she remembered, really, but Grimald all the same. His golden eyes were green now, flecked with gold, his face ruddy only from crying, and the nurse remarked that his milk teeth had fallen out since Caitlin had taken ill.

"He's fussy, 'cause he's teething. We found nothing soothes him as much as a macaroon in a little milk."

Caitlin mused on words remembered, scraps of a dream: *Be careful what you choose to tell them, for those who return from the Otherworld are never more to be believed.* Could it have been merely a dream, an overdose of ergot? The evidence in her arms, where the changeling slept as innocent as any human child, seemed undeniable. But where had the silvery mark on Caitlin's forehead come from? Fever marks were known, but not one so perfectly made. Caitlin traced the outline of it in the mirror, wondering at it. It had almost the outline of a kiss.

So Caitlin might have remembered it always, an unacknowledged and unreasoning grief driving her to madness. But then they found Fiddle.

After his brush with Ylfcwen he had fled to the cheese caves and had been hiding there ever since, only surfacing when an unvaried diet of cheese began to pall.

"Well, it solves the mystery of the larder, anyway," Iiliana said and listened with increasing astonishment as Fiddle related, over a plate of custard tarts, all that he had witnessed of Chameol's sleep.

Outside it was bitterly cold, and an unforgiving wind swung the shingle on its hinges with a mournful sound. Inside the cobbler thought she might as well take the sign down. It certainly didn't bring in any custom, and at least she would be spared having to listen to it at night.

There came a knock at the door. It was late; the cobbler had put away her work and had settled down in front of the fire with her accounts. She sighed and rose to answer the door, not very much surprised at the lateness of the call. Her creditors had been known to rouse her from her bed past midnight to demand payment.

It was not a creditor at all, but a ghost. "Mama," it said, and fell upon her neck.

In all the commotion of laughter and tears the cobbler did not notice the second figure still hanging in the doorway. Tillie finally pulled Iimogen forward. The cobbler needed no explanation and without hesitation gave Iimogen the same kiss and embrace she had bestowed on her own daughter.

"Now come in, girls, and get by the fire. Heavens, it's a bitter night, and I've kept you standing in the doorway. Come in and get into some warm things while I stir up the fire."

Her hands were so unsteady with the shock of joy that she dropped and broke the old blue teapot and burned the bread twice, but at last they were settled by the fire with tea and rarebit.

The cobbler put her hand to Tillie's cheek and traced the lines of the scratches still visible there.

"What happened to you? Did a cat do this?"

Tillie glanced at Iimogen, but the younger girl had dropped off where she sat, her face flushed from the fire, the dog licking her hand where it hung down.

"No—they're nothing more than briar scratches." Tillie rose from her chair yawning and gave her mother a kiss. "Now I think we ought to get Iimogen to bed."

Love Regained

For the first weeks of Elric's blindness, Grisaudra nursed him. She endured his ill temper and complaints with no perceptible resentment, ever silent but never cold, gentle yet not tender. He sometimes hardly knew she had been in the room, as though she were one of the invisible servants of the monster prince in a fairy tale. Elric's despair raged within him, and he struck out once, sending a bowl of compresses to the floor with a crash.

"Leave it!" he hissed through his teeth, hearing her kneel to pick up the pieces. "I'm blind; leave it! Can't you see it's useless!"

Grisaudra reached out to calm him, and at the touch of her hands on his shoulders he flailed his arms, choking with fury. "Don't touch me! Leave me—I don't want your pity!"

It was so silent for a moment he thought she had left the room. Then he heard the whisper of her clothes as she knelt again and the soft chime of the shards against each other in her hand as she gathered them up, heard the sound of the cloth wrung out at the basin. Her voice spoke at last from the doorway.

"I should have thought that you of all people, Elric, would know the difference between pity and love."

He sat alone the rest of that day, but she did not return. Love—what did she mean, love? What, love him? She could not have meant that; it was madness to consider it. But, though his mind turned her words over and over until the coals had become a heap of cold ash, Elric could winnow no other meaning from them.

At last he stumbled up from his chair and, creeping around the room, felt along the mantelpiece and cupboards until he found the matches and tinderbox. He revived the fire, filled the kettle from the pail by the door, and brewed himself some tea.

The hour was very late when he heard her come back into the room. When Elric felt her hand on his brow, testing him for fever, he quickly seized Grisaudra by the wrist and held her fast.

"What did you mean this morning?"

"You know very well. Are you so surprised?"

"No." He drew her down into the chair beside him. "I must have known for a long time, though I denied it. Imagine my dread and terror today, when I realized what was happening. And you—do you find the idea distasteful?"

In answer she took his hand and placed it over her heart so he could feel it beating swiftly as the wings of a bird. Elric ran his hands lightly over her face, wiping away her sudden tears with the side of his thumb, tracing her upper and lower lip before kissing her, as if relearning by touch what wonder was, and delight, reinventing joy. In that room time seemed to stand still, unable to touch them. The fire lay dead on the hearth, but they were not cold.

In the chair, he held Grisaudra close, smoothing and re-smoothing the warm whorl of her ear.

"You must be certain," he said at last. "My eyes may be payment enough to buy me from my vows to Chameol, but Iiliana may yet find a use for her blind knight. Could you live with that?"

Grisaudra laid her head upon his breast. "Yes. I have thought it through and through. I only worry that when you regain your sight you will change your mind. My voice is pleasing enough, but not so that it would overcome my face."

"And that is your only reservation?"

"The only one worth mentioning. We are very much alike, Elric. If we do not hate each other, what else is left for us but love?"

When the day came and Elric's eyes were unbandaged, it was still uncertain whether his sight should ever fully return. For the time being he saw dimly and greenly through a pair of thick, dark spectacles. When he was ready to travel, they set off together for Oncemoon to retrieve her belongings from the hut in the marsh.

They were camped for the night a few days from Oncemoon when Grisaudra left Elric to refill their water bottles and search the hedgerow for nests and mushrooms so they might have an omelet for their supper. She set off across the fields, stepping over the hedges and stiles, her heart light as she watched wild geese pass overhead, calling to each other. The air was sharp with cold and peat smoke from farmers' cottages.

The evening was beginning to settle down upon the gentle hills when in the failing light Grisaudra came upon a tinker's family camped in the field. Three older children ran around pulling the tail feathers of the tethered geese. Their mother shouted at them without looking up from the potatoes she was peeling, trading a remark with the grandmother, who was tending two younger children and a pig. Nearby, the father had set up a makeshift forge and was reshoeing the cart-horse.

Grisaudra hid herself, though she need not have. Her family would not have known her, even without the scar. She realized with a shock that the tinker was not her father but her eldest brother, so that her mother must be the old grannie, the younger woman, her brother's wife. And that tall girl, the one pulling the two rough-and-tumble boys apart, that must be her baby sister, Olma. . . .

They did not see her. Grisaudra moved away and quickly filled the water jug at a brooklet, realizing she had left Elric too long alone. When she got back to the place where they had made their own camp for the night, Grisaudra found Elric smoking his pipe and roasting chestnuts in the fire. She knelt beside him to warm her hands. He reached out and touched her cheek.

"You were out in the fields a long time."

"Yes."

"You're cold. Are you sure you're all right?"

Grisaudra shuddered uncontrollably. "I must have caught a chill. I had better go to sleep."

But his hands were on her face, and she could not keep Elric from reading with his fingers the high feeling written there.

"What happened? Did you see something, or is this just cold feet, now we are so close to home?"

"Oh no! Not that." She kissed him anxiously. "Not that! I ran across a band of robbers camped in the field. I don't think they saw me."

He was silent for a long moment, his hands heavy on her shoulders. "Grisaudra," he said at last. "You're free to go with them. You're not bound to me. I can make my way on my own."

"Why should I want to go off with a band of robbers?" she said, trying to make herself angry with him but failing, finding herself holding him tightly where they knelt by the fire.

"Why should you tie yourself to a blind man?"

"Hush—forget them, as they have forgotten me. They gave me up for dead long ago. Now it's my turn to lay their ghosts to rest."

Autumn had rusted the leaves of the arbor and brought a bite to the air that made it too cool to sit out, but sit out Caitlin did. She sat on the cold stone bench, a small book open in her lap, watching Bram-who-was-Grimald asleep at her feet in the wicker cradle, thinking he would soon outgrow it. Pomamber dozed nearby, one eye half-open, to see that no ravens stole the tarnished and raveled silver ribbon that marked the place in her mistress's book or the bright gilded laces that bound small bells to the baby's slippers.

While searching for a wayward hair comb, Caitlin had found the book wedged between the head of her bed and the wall. It was a girdlebook, small enough to be obscured by the flat of her hand, its covers thick with a dust that clung and glittered like crushed dragonflies' wings. The cover was set with bits of colored glass, and the clasp that bound it was cheap tin. Upon opening the book, Caitlin was annoyed to find it blank.

Iiliana had never seen it and had no idea where it could have come from.

"It's certainly not from my library. Perhaps one of the girls was making a diary. Take it; it's no earthly use to me, I'm sure."

Caitlin took it, found a pen and some ink, and began that afternoon to fill the pages with her smallest hand, stopping when the overwound spring of her script gave her hand a cramp. She meant to write out all she could remember of Ylfcwen's court etiquette. Her recall of it was already imperfect. Whole long passages, like scenes from a dream, appeared amid entries on proper elvish wedding toasts and the baking of funeral cakes. It was as though she were gazing into the mirrored surface of a pond, glimpsing beneath the glassy reflection of sky and clouds the lurk of carp and turtle.

There were few things, anymore, that she *was* certain of. The beads of wax from her taper sank to the bottom of the basin in meaningless lumps; the flames of the white tapers stretched into smoky tongues, guttered, and went out. Caitlin was forced to take her search for omens elsewhere. Every day now she left Grimald with Iiliana, and walked— sometimes to the marshes where the wild island horses appeared and disappeared among the black and wizened trees like grey and silver ghosts. Other days she wandered to the rockiest part of the sea's edge and stood for hours, listening for the mournful bark of a seal calling her name. Today the wind off the straits chilled her to the bone, and it was dark when at last she made her way back to the palace.

She found Iiliana sprawled on the carpet by the fire, teasing the baby with a bronze tassel of her hair, as if he were a cat. Iiliana needed only one look at Caitlin's lips, blue with cold, to send for an egg beaten with rum. Caitlin was made to drink it down under the queen's watchful eye and afterward to allow a balm of soothing herbs to be rubbed into her chilled limbs. Iiliana frowned at her patient.

"You'll brood yourself sick again if you're not careful."

Caitlin raked a hand through her hair. The fire and rum had warmed and numbed her, but neither they nor the balm could reach deep enough to heal the grief that really ailed her. Caitlin leaned her head on Iiliana's shoulder. "Sometimes I think I've lost my reason, my wits as well as my purpose for being."

"That's only natural. The tug of the Otherworld is strong and not easy to shake off. You were deep in the grip of the ergot, and it will be a while before you are securely back among us. For the time being, I think it would be better if you walked a little less often in the marsh and along the shore. These lonely melancholies can't be good for you."

One day, walking with Grimald in the garden, Caitlin came upon strange marks on the ground, footprints that shimmered though the frost had burned off the rest of the garden. She followed the footprints through the garden until she came to their source, an ancient trapdoor. Then Caitlin blinked and looked again, and it was only a patch of bare ground with an oddly gnarled root that resembled an iron ring.

That night she sat up late, writing in her elvish book, and fell asleep upon her pen. Caitlin woke to find her nightshirt and the blotter blooming with ink roses. Wiping a smudge from her cheek, she saw with growing astonishment that the page before her, which had been blank the night before, had been filled in her own script while she slept. This is what she read:

Gaming, Debts, and Indentureship

Gambling is a great court pastime, and most obligations acquired in this manner are repaid in story or in song, two of the most highly prized commodities. Gold and silver are rarely used. A special sort of betting is used in connection with the servitude of humans and goblins, and with human children brought into the court in an exchange. A game board of ebony is inlaid with gems to represent the gemfields of the Otherworld, and the indentured is represented by a carved piece of wood or stone. Through skill and chance the player must complete a circuit of the board in a given number of moves, without landing on the region of the board claimed for the queen. If a player lands on a square without a number, he merely loses the game. Should a player land on a square bearing a number, however, the player's servitude is extended by a corresponding number of years.

When she had read it, Caitlin's memory of all that had passed in Drusian's chamber returned, and she knew the meaning of the passage. The seer of Chameol laid her head on her arms and wept, for her memory regained and for the son she had lost.

Iiliana started at the sight of the man in the doorway. He was dressed in the dark, close-fitting clothes of a highwayman, the black cloth silvered with a crust of saltwater. Seen from the darkened doorway, his eyes were a startling blue in a face the shadows made dark as a miner's. The eyes told Iiliana all she needed to know. The queen crossed the room swiftly, as if to embrace him. Then she saw the crown in his hand and the cloak over his arm and fell to her knees, afraid to ask the price that had been paid for them.

The Badger spoke through lips blistered by the wind and sun. "Myrrhlock is no more." He placed his burdens, the one shining, the other seeming to gather to it all the light, at Iiliana's feet and then sank to the floor, all his strength gone. Iiliana raised her eyes, a silent question written in her features.

"Elric lives," the Badger said. "But he gave his sight, Iiliana. I left him in the hands of a capable nurse."

Iiliana shed the last thread of her queenly demeanor and burst into tears of mingled sorrow and relief. The Badger let her weep for a time before he asked the question most on his own mind.

"Where is she?"

He found Caitlin asleep. The book had fallen shut in her lap, and the hood of her cloak had slipped back, loosing her hair to the wind, which teased it out in tendrils around her face. The Badger crouched the better part of an hour among the leaves of the arbor, afraid to wake her and find that he was asleep himself and this was but another dream. So rapt was he that it was some minutes before he noticed the cradle at her feet.

"I *am* dreaming," he muttered, stepping forward from his hiding place and gingerly lifting the swaddled child from the wicker cradle. One look at Grimald's golden-green eyes and slightly pointed ears and the Badger knew this was his mooncalf, his firstborn son.

"Hello!" he said under his breath. "And who are you?"

"His name is Grimald."

Caitlin was sitting up, rubbing the kinks from her neck, her eyes roaming over the changes his absence had made in the Badger, the way his eyes seemed polished with sleeplessness, the restless poise of his limbs, ready to flee: the marks of a knight of Chameol or someone haunted by a ghost.

The Badger could not tear his eyes from her face. Even flushed from sleep, Caitlin's features were suffused with a tender sorrow that made her lovely to behold. For a long moment, beholding her was all he could to do. At last the Badger stepped forward and placed Grimald in Caitlin's arms.

"A funny name for a baby. Better for an old man than a boy. But it suits him. How did you choose it?" While the Badger said this, he cautiously twined the fingers of his hand in Caitlin's.

"He named himself, in an odd way," she replied so softly that he hardly heard her. Her fingers closed around his. "Do you know the thing for which I will never forgive myself?" she said suddenly. "Sending you away the way I did, without telling you how much I loved you."

At that he broke down and wept.

Iiliana barred the household from the hallway leading to Caitlin's rooms, but the precaution was unnecessary. Upon retiring, the Badger fell soundly asleep and spent the night of their reunion in the most profound slumber he had enjoyed in a year, while Pomamber guarded Grimald in his cradle at the foot of the bed.

But Caitlin slept less soundly. Toward dawn she dreamed of Ylfcwen's court and of the room where mortal interlopers wove tapestries to color and warm the walls of elvish stone. A weaver was working on a tapestry of a monastery. Looking over his shoulder, Caitlin could see the beehives, the stables, and, off behind the garden wall, the orange grove. Here was the stableboy, asleep under a tree, and a fat monk hurrying up to summon him to prayers. Caitlin knew the weaver before the dream showed his face: It was the Badger. His face was pale and blank with hopelessness, and his hands worked the loom mechanically.

The dream showed the approach of a jeweled foot and an intricate hem; attired so regally, who could it be but Ylfcwen? An ivory hand reached out and came to rest on the Badger's shoulder, a gesture of possessiveness, not of lover to beloved, but of master to pet.

"When you are finished with this one, bring it to my chamber," said the queen.

"Yes, milady." Eyes followed the elf queen's retreat down the hall, eyes as blue with scorn as the sapphires on the train of her gown.

But the figure they followed was Caitlin.

The Badger woke to find Caitlin crouching on the cold floor, her knees drawn up, wracked with silent sobs. At once he was beside her, his arms around her, kissing her face through the screen of her hair. He helped her back into the bed and settled her among the pillows.

"It was awful," she whispered.

"Tell me."

In halting but unsparing words she related her dream. When she finished, her eyes were glazed with tears, her mouth a grimace of pain. "Get out, go, before I make you hate me—"

"Caitlin." He smoothed the hair gently from her face. "I couldn't hate you, any more than I could forget you. Not that I didn't do my best. But when I tried, every part of me rebelled against it, Cait. I love you. I have to live my life beside you. You must believe that."

She could only nod her head mutely. He kissed her lightly on her mouth.

"It was so real," she murmured.

"No," he said, pulling her close. "This is."

The Badger knew there were nightmares in his past he could never bring himself to share with her. His own turn would come, he knew, to wake in the night, the name of fear on his lips. But they would neither of them wake alone, ever again.

Caitlin woke late in the morning without first remembering her nightmare and lay awhile sleepily, thinking the Badger and his words part of a dream.

Then she remembered and turned to watch him dreaming beside her. Her eyes roamed over him, noting the creases care had carved beneath his eyes, the way his mouth was soft with sleep, the new beard glittering on his jaw. Then Caitlin saw on his wrist the bracelet of her hair, plaited so tightly it gleamed as smooth and polished as steel. She shuddered, thinking of manacles and bells, and slipped from the bed without waking him.

Hello, she mouthed to Grimald in his wicker cradle. Grimald made an *O* of his mouth back at her. She placed her finger to her mouth, miming for silence, picked up the changeling, and carried him to Iiliana's rooms.

Iiliana was at her dresser, her bronze hair unbound and streaming over her shoulders. She looked up as Caitlin came in and waved her to a seat on the bed.

"There's something on the tray by the bed, if you're hungry. I haven't looked yet."

Caitlin lay on her back, holding Grimald overhead. He didn't crow, like most babies, but his golden-green eyes got wider and wider. Caitlin kissed him and set him down. The tray held a pitcher of milk and a plate of rolls. She tore a roll in two, dipped one half in milk before giving it to Grimald, and ate the other.

Iiliana finished dressing her hair and turned to Caitlin. "How are you this morning?"

Caitlin did not answer immediately. "If I had to answer only for today—then, happy."

"And for tomorrow?"

Caitlin shook her head. "I'm afraid. How can it work? My work is here, while as a man he can't even remain on the island. Not to mention the vows he took as a knight of Chameol." She laughed. "It's like the plot to a penny romance. Star-crossed, and then some."

"Mmm." Iiliana frowned hard at the tray before picking up the jam pot and a spoon. "I'll say two things, then—with my mouth full. First, he already loves that child, and you're sadly mistaken if you think you'll be able to separate them. Second, Chameol is not the island she was anymore. She can't be, now we know of Iule. I think the days of our cloister are over and that the vows of our knights must be reviewed." Iiliana put another spoonful of jam into her mouth and looked into Caitlin's startled eyes with an expression of utmost innocence.

EIGHTEEN

The Boy
with Amber Eyes

*T*he Direwolves watched the progress deeper into the Weirdwood of a dog and three humans: a mated pair and a youngling. The mingled scents, human and goblin, confused the watchers, and they sat back on their haunches, keen-eyed but not venturing any nearer.

Caitlin walked a little ahead, carrying the bundle with the small jeweled book and a few other volumes from Chameol's library, Iiliana's gifts to them on the occasion of their wedding and leave-taking. Caitlin had chosen first a book on the powers and properties of stones, and second, a bestiary—chiefly for the quaint and cunning pictures of seals that the monk, who must once have been a sailor, had added to the margins of the text. For his part, the Badger had chosen a treatise on the treatment of various equine maladies and an encyclopedia of common childhood ailments. For these he had passed up a book with wonderful color plates of a joust and had lingered only briefly over an atlas with folding maps the size of tablecloths.

"It's a different sort of life we're going to," he had said to Caitlin, showing her his choices rather sheepishly.

Though what use he hoped to make of the horse book in the Weirdwood, Caitlin couldn't imagine. His beloved piebald, Motley, was to remain behind on Chameol to bring fresh blood to the stock of horses that ran wild in the marshes. The dappled horse had wickered a good-bye into his master's neck, mouthing his hair as if it were part of the farewell offering of meadow-sweet hay.

The horse would not have liked the Weirdwood; the grasping branches of the trees, the watchfulness of owls would not have agreed with Motley at all, the Badger thought as he followed Caitlin, carrying Grimald before him snug in a bunting. Caitlin's dark cloak made it hard to see her as she slipped with native ease through the trees, and the Badger was glad of the mastiff, one of Pomamber's daughters.

Caitlin had been afraid she would not be able to find it, but every twig and stone seemed to know her and point the way.

"Here," she said, coming to a stop in a clearing and turning in a slow circle. "It should be right—there!"

The red door was green with moss, but the key was where she had left it, under a stone. Inside, the house of her childhood was gone, and in its place was a ruin looted not by human hands but by squirrels and owls and time; mattresses spilled rotting straw, drawers were turned out, porcelain jars smashed, the tiles of the hearth dug up in a search for nuts. In the pantry, jars of mushrooms, ground roots, and dried lizards were tumbled everywhere, and what had not been eaten had been taken for nest material.

Caitlin leaned her head on the Badger's shoulder.

"I didn't expect it to be this bad."

"Well," he said thoughtfully, glancing around. "I've cleaned many a stall in my day. It's not so bad. First thing we do, let's light a fire."

By the time it was dark they had a livable room, beaten, swept, and scoured. They laid a cloth on the floor by the hearth, until the chairs could be mended, and made a supper out of cheese and dried apples. On the old bookstand the repaired book of incantations lay in stately repose, and if Abagtha's spirit was still in that house, it was appeased.

Caitlin drowsed, Grimald in her arms, the Badger's arms

around her. The upper room would become hers, and she planned to outfit it for her new task: reconstructing the five Books of the Keepers. She would sell spells and remedies enough to buy all the books she required. Against the other wall she would fix a niche for her candles and basins and other tools of divination. And she wanted to add a window to look out through the branches to the sky and stars and, not least of all, to admit pigeons bearing news of Chameol.

The old root cellar was to be the Badger's, and he had already measured it out in paces and found it large enough to hold a small printing press. Mending tack had made him handy with a needle, and he meant to try his hand at making books.

The Badger shook Caitlin awake gently, kissing her ear. "It's late—"

Outside, the Direwolves settled down in their dens contentedly. Things were well: Magic had returned to the Weirdwood. The owls nodded their agreement, and the wind in the trees muttered about it.

In the oak with the red door, the Badger had made up the bed and placed Grimald in the middle of it. Caitlin climbed in after, yawning as she took down her hair. The Badger sat on the edge of the bed, kicking off his boots.

"I meant to ask you before, Cait. What is that trapdoor in the cellar?"

But Caitlin was already asleep.

Ulfra stood before the window, looking out into the filthy streets of Moorsedge. A little towheaded boy, just Nix's size a year ago, was running up the street with some apples he had stolen from under the apple-seller's nose. Ulfra let the curtain fall.

The leopard-woman looked up from her sewing. "Why

don't you take a walk? You can finish those hems later."

Ulfra shook her head. "I haven't done my lessons today."

Tansy shrugged. "Suit yourself. There's cold mutton, if you want it; the joint end's rarer, the way you like it. You can have it at the little table, by the fire."

The girl (the wolf had nearly gone out of her) cut herself some meat and bread and settled down by the fire with her paper and pencil. It was certainly easier to get wolves to jump through hoops than to get a pencil to go in the direction you wanted it to go. She copied out some sentences and fell to staring raptly at the fire and at the way it made the deep marmalade-colored stuff of her dress glow like fire itself. Ulfra still preferred trousers, and she liked to put her hair up under a cap and take the dog out for a long walk, searching all the lanes and hedges, though she never meant to, for a small boy with white hair.

The letters flew up in the air; the silver letter opener and letter tray clattered to the floor. The courtier hurriedly knelt and began to collect the scattered correspondence.

"There is *one* thing, madam, that demands your attention."

Ylfcwen arched an eyebrow at *demands.* "Leave them," she said, removing her pet mole from a pigeonhole of her writing desk. It snuggled sleepily into her hand. "I'll read them later. But first I shall have a bath."

Elves do not need to bathe, the *Elvish Book of Court Etiquette* tells us; they lack the glands to make it a necessity, and life Below makes the practice impractical. For the queen, however, almost anything could be arranged, and there was a little-used chamber where hot springs had been piped into a tiled pool. This was hastily scoured and filled, some orchid crystals found, and a large, soft robe recovered from an old wedding chest.

Ylfcwen settled into the water happily. At Emma's, even having to boil her own water and lug the heavy kettle up the stairs to the tub, she had taken no fewer than three baths a day. The discovery of bathing almost made up for the loss of both Bram and Grimald.

She got out before her wings were too waterlogged and left a trail of silvery wet footprints the length of the hall to her room. There, in the center of the bed, lay the thing that most demanded the elf queen's attention.

He was pink and plump with health; she gave him a good pinch to see that there was nothing wrong with his lungs. Then Ylfcwen lifted Bram squalling into her arms, an unaccustomed smile tugging at one corner of her mouth.

"Well, little raven, we must see if we can find you a nice rattle."

Epilogue

"Nix!"

At the woodpile Nix wedged the ax into the chopping block, seized an armful of kindling, and ran with it back to the house. Seven years of Mistress Goody's amazing and wonderful soup could not make him big, but he had grown wiry and strong for his size.

"Oh, good, you remembered the kindling. Just put it in the box and hurry up. We're taking this lot in to market, and you're to help me with the stall."

They loaded the cart with sausages, hams, and crocks of pickles and jam. Mistress Goody liked to have Nix along when she took her goods to market; he could make change quick as a wink and always knew which customer had slipped an extra sausage into her marketing basket. She loved the boy as well as she did any of her other children, and it worried her that she had never heard him laugh, though when asked he always denied that he was unhappy. Well, the boy had always been a mystery, as unexpected though welcome as the money that arrived anonymously for him every month to keep him in shoes and coats, and as the bundle of dresses that had arrived once for her and all the girls.

They got a stall in an excellent location and set out their wares. Soon the marketplace was abustle with early-morning marketers, and Mistress Goody and Nix were kept very busy until eleven o'clock. Things had just slowed down when two wealthy women came up to the stall, one wearing a hat that veiled her face, her arm linked with that of her companion, a woman whose bright gaze danced from under the brim of her fashionable hat. The companion pointed to the Goodys' stall with an elegant, gloved hand.

"Oh, look, Tansy. Sausages! Shall we get some? I'm tired of partridge; we'll dine on sausages and beans tonight."

The voice that issued from behind the veil had a light lisp. "Yes, but let me; I haven't haggled in a long time."

While Tansy began to bargain with Mistress Goody, her pretty companion began to turn over the crocks of preserves. "How much are these?" she asked, without looking up.

"Tuppence," Nix whispered hoarsely around the heart sticking in his throat.

It was then Ulfra looked up and gazed for a long time at the wondrous and amazing changes time had made in her Nix. At last she smiled and drew a gold coin from her purse.

"I'll take two of the plum and one of the pear, please."

It was that seventh year also that a boy came out of nowhere, a boy just Grimald's height, with raven-dark hair and amber eyes. Caitlin found him when she was out gathering mushrooms, the silvery, fragile kind that spring up in the night and are gone by the time the sun is very high. She came upon the boy curled asleep in a pile of leaves, his face stained with tears.

Caitlin brought him back to the oak with the red door and fed him, but she did not ask him too many questions, knowing all she needed for the moment from the silver ring on his finger, the muddy amber of his eyes. They took him in and treated him as their son. Grimald was not pleased at the start with this intruder, but the rivalry faded in time. His new companion was awfully good at digging moles from their burrows and always knew where to find a cave to play in, and Grimald began to believe having a brother was not such a bad thing after all.